TEFLON BLACC

# NAME OF DA GAME

For more information, email nameofdagame@gmail.com

**Printed in the United States of America**
Available from https://www.nameofdagame.com and other retail outlets

**First Printing Edition, 2021**
ISBN: 979-8-9907900-1-8

# NAME OF DA GAME

# 3.5 Grams

## AUGUST 26, 2005

There I lay in the bed barely opening my eyes as the bright sun peeked through the curtains.

"Good morning, babe" Ashanti greeted me as she came back through the bedroom doorway.

"Hey good morning, bae" I replied as she leaned across the bed giving me a series of kisses. She started to rub her hand over the top of my chest and kissed me as her hands kept creeping south. She gripped my dick and popped him in her mouth as I started to grow. He grew instantly as she slurped and bobbed until it hit the back of her throat. She paused for a second to catch her breath and spit on the tip. I watched it roll down the shaft hitting her hand. She licked it off her knuckles and headed back up to the tip to put me in her mouth.

# NAME OF DA GAME

While bobbing up and down she moaned and let the saliva burst out of her mouth. She popped her wrist while in motion. She kept going while flipping her body in between my legs. She looked in my eyes while the spit covered her mouth. I pulled her hand away from the dick and pushed down on her head. She started to gag then came up to catch her breath before she tried to attack my manhood again, whole.

"Suck daddy's dick bae." I said talking my shit and encouraging her on to keep it up. Once she gagged, I grabbed her by her arms and made her climb on top as I straightened my legs out. My hands gripped on her waist catching her rotation each time while I grinded from the bottom too. She kept spinning around on her dirty wind.

"Oh my God, Daddy I love it." She blurted out before I gripped up under her thighs and started to nail her from the bottom once I planted my feet in the mattress. She immediately started to moan loud as hell as I had found my rhythm. I was crashing her body with force into mines. She was looking up with her eyes and her mouth was stuck wide open.

"Naw, take this dick bae." I told her as I could feel her trying to slow down and her body tensing up. This took place for a few minutes before I tapped the side of the bed signaling for her to lay down on her back.

I was unsure if she was going to try to push me off or pull me in closer while I sucked on the clit. I was gripping her legs up in the air so she couldn't move them giving a few wet firm licks so I could get directly to the clit. She took it like a g as I did what I wanted.

"Oh babe, oh babe, oh my gawd, what the fuck!" She shouted as my face went crazy on her lady parts.

"Oh shit!" she shouted as she forcefully slipped away once again.

"Fuck you going? I ain't done." I said talking my shit, she darted out the room heading to the living room. I popped up right behind her giving chase and getting my timbs along the way.

"Ewww shit, fuck me, daddy fuck me, faster, harder, uh, uh…." my girl Ashanti shouted as I drilled her from the back picking up the pace the more she ran her mouth. I had her bent over the black leather loveseat in our living room.

"Daddy don't stop I'm about to cum." she said out loud as she reached her hand back gripping my hip. I kept going using full force. I was giving her all and more as she screamed and collapsed onto the edge of the couch. Her pussy throbbed as it hugged my dick. I grinded slowly until I busted warmly inside her.

"Beep, Beep, Beep" went my squawky. I had just finished cleaning myself off as Ashanti came bringing me my phone. "I didn't look to see who it is, but Pimp is parked right out front, so I wouldn't be surprised," said Ashanti.

"Yo" I said as I squawked in.

"I'm outside Neph." Pimp squawked back.

I grabbed my shirt and beater from Ashanti as I gave her a kiss. I gripped her ass and pulled her close while telling her goodbye. Now Ashanti was a star in my eyes for sure. She was petite, about 5'6", and had a brown skinned complexion. Baby girl was stacked with a nice apple bottom and weighed about 150 even. She's a smart girl in beauty school for cosmetology and fashion design. Her ambition and her grind turn me on the most.

Some people called her a baby cougar since I'm only 16 and she's 24. I don't see it that way at all. I'm just a young nigga with swag and she got good taste. I'm a little cocky when it comes to me and that's just who I am. I'm 5'10, dark skinned, with a muscular frame. My six pack was right and my tats on full throttle all over my arms and chest. I'm the truth and I have a good head on my shoulders too. I dropped out of high school six months ago and received my GED. So now I have my days to myself to wake up every day to get money. Shit honestly, that's all I know. By the way, my name is Shawn Rodgers, but everybody calls me "Sales".

See we don't do government names in my city of Pittsburgh, Pennsylvania. We leave that for the cops. I earned my name because I been making sales since I jumped off the porch in 2000. The first time I ever fucked up the money I was flipping some smoke. It was like my fourth flip. I was trying to buy everything like I was the man. The second time I was about age thirteen. I got robbed for my crack by some grown motherfuckers from across town.

I ain't let it break a real nigga's stride. I just took the little money I had left and started pumping weed in school. I was banking close to $600 a day until I got caught. They put me on juvenile probation. That just made me learn from my mistakes. Now me and Ashanti have our game plan together and we gone make it.

I been fuckin with Pimp the whole time me and Ashanti been together. We been down for 11 months and living together for eight of them. Around the hood we refer to Pimp as a "Big Gate". He got that bread. He's real selective with who and how he moves though. He might put you up on game, but that's only if he feels you got it all in the right spots. You know, balls, determination and a cold heart.

"What's up Unc?" I greeted as I opened the door to Pimp's money green two door Eldorado and taking a seat.

"What's up Neph? My name Pimping, right? Yeah, so I had to cut off Star and Stormy Street's stalking asses. These bitches are playing for the wrong team. I'm just making sure your playbook is in order." Pimp said. He paused for a second to make sure I was following along before continuing on.

"Stop past A first, drop off at C, then pick up at F", said Pimp. He always took extra precautions to have a game plan as he redirected me on how my re-up was going to go.

"Iight bet" I replied.

"Iight now you know the name of da game, right? Go on get out." said Pimp as he put his car in drive waiting for me to get out. I exited his vehicle and felt he was my pimp or something. Every single time we talked his mouthpiece was sly as fuck.

"Hey babe, are you ready?" I asked as I stuck my head through the front door. I walked out to our 02' Bonneville which I got painted and detailed my favorite color cocaine. Yes, everything is white from the interior, tires, to wood grain in the dashboard. I even got a custom white flip out touchscreen TV too. White is just so sexy and to me it means money – just like cocaine.

## "Supply & Demand"

I dropped Ashanti off at beauty school and made my rounds around the city. I usually went to pick up my little bro Don-D. We resembled each other in a lot of ways. He was my complexion and my height as well. He wasn't biologically my brother. We did grow up on the same block though. We lived just a few doors down from each other on Lincoln Ave.

We shared the same birthday too just a year apart. People often would mistake us for blood because we're both built the same too. I never did mind the assumption since my parents were killed by a drunk driver. I was only four years old, but it was the most tragic moment of my life. I was an only child and always wanted a brother growing up. Me and Don-D just always ended up being there for each other. Literally through it all.

Knock knock, I hit his mom's door before walking in. They never locked doors in their household. Nor were they ever robbed or had anyone try to ever hit the crib up. I always figured it was because of how his dad, Big Sherm got pull in the hood.

Big Sherm went away 5 years ago to the feds. His connect turned pussy and snitched on him. Somebody gave up the connect first but that's still some fuck boy shit. After a year-long investigation they found him guilty and sentenced him to 121 months. He never had any priors so he can be home in 2010, so I heard.

"Momma Mase, how are you today?" I asked as I seen her sitting on the couch doing her daughter Nevaeh's hair. She was only 5 years old.

"Hey Sales, how are you baby? Don is back in the kitchen." she replied as I greeted them both with hugs and kisses. Then I headed back through their four-bedroom townhouse to find bro. It was such a nice crib too.

Now Momma Macy was only 32 years old. If you do the math, she was 16 when she had Don-D. She was chocolate like us with flawless skin. She was thick like ATL strippers working in Magic City. She's bad and all the big-time moneymakers in the city wanted her. She could definitely pull them all too. Listen, the Wall Street executives, lawyers, jack boys and the top kingpins all want her. But she has her king already in Big Sherm and doesn't even fuck around. That's one reason why I love and respect her so much. Her loyalty is unmatched.

"What's good bro?" Don-D asked as he was lacing up his white-on-white Air Max 95's that matched his polo shirt.

"Shit, trying to get this money. What's good? Are you ready?" I asked.

"Yeah, yup we out." he said jumping up with a grin on his face.

Don-D was my right hand, but he wasn't full blooded with this shit. He was only doing it until he could start making some money from his football dreams. I respected that so I made sure he was away from eye's view as much as possible. Making sure he was safe, was my priority. Shit I took better care of him than myself. You know that's loyalty though. And that I always was.

"Come on bro, what are you doing?" I asked as I seen Don-D pulling out the keys to his '98 Tahoe. Since he was my bro, I got it painted cocaine for him. He put some 22" inch deep dish players on them. "I'm going to park in Lexi's garage because I ain't coming back over this way tonight." Don-D said referring to Ashanti's lil sister as we both chuckled.

"She still ain't giving you no pussy nigga." I said laughing at him. Mr. Morris Chestnut has been trying to fuck for close to a year now and she still ain't with it.

"Nigga she gone give me some pussy or I'll pay for it." Don-D said as we both laughed. We hopped in our rides and headed towards Lexi's house.

After dropping off Don-D's truck it was time to stop past Spot A. Pimp's sister lives there. It ain't never anything there and won't ever be. If something were to ever go down that would be the first spot to be hit because of the traffic in and out. That way we stayed aware of any law enforcement or jack boys trying to come up the easy way. It was pure genius if you asked me. She was licensed to carry and on disability but never goes anywhere.

After stopping there for about 5 minutes it was time to stop at Spot C which was Chocolate City. That's Pimp's nightclub that he lets these Jewish people run. Mainly so his face isn't in the spotlight. He clocks numbers through there every night.

See we still fuckin with that coke and getting them so low. They come in at $800 an ounce and we're paying $3500 for 4.5 ounces. We break them down, rock them up and sell them to fiends. We are looking at an average of $2800. That's a $2,000 profit per ounce. Listen, do the math correctly and it's a net total of $12,600 easily. It will only take us a few days maximum to make that.

This is why I love this country. Only in America can you have something so small equal to something so great. Supply and demand coupled with where we had it booming at was everything. Not too many shorts came through there. If they did, that was my touter's problems, with it being one of them spot where point one goes for the dub. It definitely ain't my issue because my money comes first. They kept whatever was extra over the top for themselves. Shit, that's just the way life is.

After we stopped there, it was time to go to spot F. That's the McDonalds in East Liberty Penn Circle. Drop offs were usually made in the parking lots and bathrooms of busy areas for safety precautions. We usually kept our eyes out on the cars that were too anything. It could be too distant or too close. If it rode by and was too common or frequent; we kept a close eye on it. And especially if it kept making the same turns. We stayed on point because the streets are always watching.

"You got them?" Don-D asked as I got back in the ride.

"Yeah, yup we gone weigh it soon as we get to Auntie's crib." I replied.

"Cool, because she been hitting me up too. She said she only got a few grizzlies left."

"Well as long as all our money there, that ain't going to be no problem." I replied. No matter how much money she makes us at the end of the day she still a snizzy.

I turned up the Trap or Die mix tape by Young Jeezy. I heard this shit for the first time 4 months ago. That's what really made me turn it up to the tenth power. It makes you want to get key fare and break it all down into point everything and repeat the flow. Just to get every dollar that you deserve. The way I'm feeling right now I just might do that. I seriously might. I'm always in stack mode so I don't spend much. I feel really prepared just in case. I got 25k set aside for lawyers and bail fees. I got 10k for my birthday in a couple days. I got 30k buried in my Nana's basement. And it's close to 20k in arms reach between two homes.

If I can get another 8 months strong out of the game, I might be set for life. If not for life, it will at least open the door to establish my brand. I'm a businessman at heart. I want a beauty salon, tattoo parlor, and auto body shop. I also want a clothing store and to invest in real estate. I don't plan to execute everything at the same time. The goal is to build the board like Monopoly. I'm on some true serial entrepreneur shit. The skill of my hustle surpasses beyond the street game. That's only the tip of the iceberg. Money always makes money. Once I come up, I plan to give back to my hood for the kids too.

"Auntie, unlock the door. We're out front." Don-D said on his phone as we pulled up to an apartment building called Carnegie Towers. It's one of those buildings that has security in the lobby. They ask for your ID and inquire about your presence in the building. Most of the time they're not even around. The security workers we do see on the regular, all get high. In my head, it's like my modern-day version of New Jack City's "Da Carter". Just like Pookie, it only took one person to fuck up something great.

"Hey there auntie, how you doing?" I asked as I entered the door solo. This was always for precautionary measures. I made sure nobody was here trying to throw any type of party for us. I don't trust anybody as far as I can throw them. The first thing Pimp taught me when we hooked up was you learn your surroundings. Being aware helps you stay on point. Always have an alternate route to leave and know the best way to travel to escape. Mainly because anything can happen. We have to stay on point to do what's necessary to avoid getting caught.

"Hey Baby, now where's my other one at?" Auntie Michelle asked as she cracked open her a can of Coors Light before giving me a hug.

"He's on his way up the steps. You know he's a slow ass walker." I replied as I walked to the bathroom.

I grabbed my big Rubbermaid gloves from under the sink and grabbed a sauce pot, a glass pyrex, a spoon, and a butter knife. Which was the same ones I usually used when it was time to cook it up. I went to the hallway closet and grabbed what I needed. That's where I kept newspaper, grocery bags, hammers, and my digital scale. The Coc usually be in chunks and have to break it down to be able to do my thing with it.

"Hey Baby, I thought you got lost for a minute. I was just asking your brother about you." Auntie said as she gave him a hug.

She proceeded to put all the locks on the door. As far as she knew we were brothers. She thinks I'm Kevin and Don-D is Keith.

This ain't our side of town so they don't need to know a motherfucking thing. And if shit ever goes sour, they won't know who we really are.

"Iight, here's the run down. Ima take care of Auntie and you whip it up." I said, filling Don-D in on what I wanted to take place. I taught Don-D how to cook up, but he still wasn't that sharp. I figured I'd keep him going at it so he could have it on smash, or a tool to always make money because a lot of people can't cook themselves, so they'll always need somebody.

"Iight bet" Don-D replied.

"Well good because y'all right on time. I'm about to run down to the lobby and sell my last four dubs. Y'all money is in my bedroom in the shoebox. Kevin, have me ready when I come back. I'm locking the door and I have my key." said Auntie as she locked both locks and exited the door going along her merry way. Don-D went to the bedroom to count the money while I weighed and broke down the chunks of cocaine on the newspaper.

"It's all here bro." Don-D shouted back into the kitchen.

"Iight, that's a bet. Bro you trying to come in here and start whipping just in case we running behind on time? It's already quarter 'til 1 and Ashanti get out of school at 4." I asked as I pulled out my cell phone checking all the missed calls from her. See she was my partner who kept me up on game and sane. The main one who always had my back with support. I feel that's why I go so hard for us. I want us to have the best life possible.

I took a sprinkle of soft dropping it on a spoon then sat it on top of the counter. As I finished Auntie came back in the apartment. I held the spoon for her as she added a pinch of baking soda. I held the lighter underneath as she took the tip of her pen and quickly made her a blast once wetting her fingers and dripping the cold water on the spoon locking the cocaine into a crack rock.

"Yeah, that's it, babm oy." she said after a big hit from her glass pipe. She staggered back into the chair directly behind her while she tried to still hold her breath before finally exhaling.

# NAME OF DA GAME

"Yeah yup, we in here bro." I said as I took her crack pipe upside down and tapping the table with it just to make sure nothing was still in there. See I liked her because she wasn't just an ordinary crack head. I referred to her as a smoker which is a functional addict who hasn't lost it. She just likes to smoke hard as her drug of choice.

Personally, I only smoke weed but not all day like pot heads. I only smoke in the comfort of my own home with my girl when I'm in for the night just chilling. I'm not with the other shit. I have to be out here on point. I can't afford any slip-ups or mistakes of any sort. That could ultimately cost me what I'm not so willing to give up which is my freedom, life, or money.

After Don-D finished his microwave magic it was time to roll. Just that quick he turned that 4 and a half into 6 ounces. We left 3 of them with auntie. We only wanted the money for two and a half. She kept the other half for herself. That's what we do for her all the time.

Our chemistry is so strong together because we treat her exceptionally well. We basically just gave $1400 away to her. By doing that we eliminated the risk. She knows she is safe, paid, and high. When you treat them good it's an incentive for them to do the same for you. We all win, and that's how one hand washes the other.

"I'm the realist nigga in it,

You already know,

Got trapper of the year 4 times in a row,

And what they give you?

A lifetime supply baking soda clientele,

A rollie watch, 2 pots & 3 scales" I shouted out loud along with the Young Jeezy verse. I drove us over to Lexi's house to drop Don-D off to meet back at my house. He was headed there while I went and picked up Ashanti from beauty school.

The plan was for me to get dropped off so she could head to the mall. She was heading to get her nails and feet done. I knew she was going to end up doing some kind of shopping because she had a couple hundred on her. She's either coming home with groceries, clothes, or something for the house. I just know without a doubt that she's buying something.

Getting in the house and counting out money with my right hand mans is always a thrill for me. Especially while watching some shit like Belly or Scarface. It's like what they are doing in the movie we are living out in real life.

"This is the life bro." I said to Don-D as I picked up my half. I headed to my bedroom to put it in my shoebox with the rest of my money in there.

"You right it definitely doesn't get no better than this money in my hand. They say young niggas don't be knowing the game. Shit nigga we make it happen." Don-D replied as he picked up his bankrolls with a big smile on his face.

He parlayed around with me for a minute. We sat and talked about our future goals for about another hour while the movie played. Don-D left for the night heading back over to Lexi's house. That's where he planned to spend the rest of the night.

I jumped in the shower and ordered some Chinese food from the China Inn in East Liberty. I got out and set everything up for our night. While I was rolling a blunt of purple haze Ashanti came walking in the house with both fists full of bags.

"Babe I did some shopping and picked us up some outfits for your birthday. It's only a few days away so I had to get you right." Ashanti said as she smiled and placed the bags on the couch across from me.

"Yeah? So, what you get?" I asked. She then pulled everything out showing me as we sat there."

"Yeah, that shit hot baby girl. I'm gone wear my gold herringbone with that." I replied as she came over to me hopping on my lap and kissing me passionately. She got up showing me her black one-piece and her black 6-inch stiletto heels.

"We'll definitely be the life of the party." I said as I walked to the front door to meet the delivery guy. Ashanti was undressing down to her red laced bra and panties as I walked back in with our food. She had a tat across her breast that read "That Bitch". Her other tat showed the paw prints leading up her right thigh up to her pussy lips which was enough to drive a grown man insane.

"Come here girl." I said in a low deep voice. I grabbed her hand as I flopped down on the couch next to her gently pulling her panties. She came over and got on top of me.

We were kissing as we caressed each other. You could tell I was giving her all types of feelings inside. I could feel the warmth from between her legs. She slowly grinded on my 8-inch rock hard dick through my hoop shorts. I held her close letting her know mentally that she was in tune with a man who wanted her mind, body, and soul. I wanted her in all the right ways. It was never just about the sex with her. My left hand never missed a beat as I unhooked her bra. We kissed and grinded slowly on each other just enjoying each other in the moment.

"Take it all off." I whispered in between kisses. She stood right up never taking her eyes off mine. She dropped her panties while I undressed myself as well.

Ashanti eagerly got back on top of me straddling my lap. She directed my manhood inside of her while I caressed her breasts. I slowly began sucking and licking on both of them. She let out sweet moans in my ear while she cradled my head in both of her arms.

"Take your time with her big daddy." she whispered in my ear. She loved biting and sucking on my bottom lip. "Oh my God Shawn!" Ashanti yelled out loud as she leaned back holding on to both of my shoulders. She grinded aggressively on my dick as I rotated in the other direction Our bodies met with each circular motion she made.

"Damn daddy, fuck!!" Ashanti moaned as we continued.

"Put your legs on my shoulders." I told her as I threw her legs up. I cuffed my arms around her shoulders while she wrapped her hands behind my head before I stood up.

"Oh fuck!!" Ashanti screamed as her eyes lit up as I went balls deep. She felt every inch of my slow but powerful thrusts inside. She let out a passionate squeak and from there I went all in. I started fuckin the shit out her in mid-air but with a slow grind to it. She started gripping her nails into the back of my neck. and for like a good ten minutes we grinded like Jamaicans. I bust like crazy inside of her. I stood there holding her as sweat dripped down my body and onto hers while giving her some out of the blue strokes until my dick went soft inside her. Then I placed her motionless body on the couch. Her whole body was shaking.

She got up after about 10 minutes and we showered together. We finished the rest of our nightcap smoking a blunt. We ate and watched re-runs of Martin until we both fell asleep on the couch.

## "It is what it is."

W aking up in the morning early was a normal thing for me. My body won't let me sleep past 7:30 am no matter what time I go to bed. Ashanti was the same way. We be up and moving all times in the morning.

"Bitch who the fuck is this? You're calling my man's phone!" yelled Ashanti. I could hear her all the way in the living room. I walked into the kitchen to see what this shit was all about.

"Bitch and what the fuck you want with him?" Ashanti said to the girl on the other end. She started grilling me and put the phone on speaker.

"Oh, you must be the one everybody keeps saying he left me and my baby for." The girl on the phone blurted out before I cut her off.

"Look hoe don't be calling my fuckin jack disrespectful and shit. First off, Kayla we ain't fucked in over a year. I damn sure wouldn't give you any hope by nutting in your stupid ass. You smut bitch lose my number", I said before snatching the phone out of Ashanti's hand and hanging it up. She immediately called right back multiple times attempting to get me to pick up her calls which I ignored. I tossed the phone down on the couch and headed back to the kitchen to get my pop-tarts out of the toaster. I watched out the corner of my eye as Ashanti followed me to the kitchen.

"Sales so you weren't fuckin her"? Ashanti asked me.

"Naw" I responded calmly.

"So why would she try to say her baby is yours then?"

"Because bitches are evil and they like to lie. You know that they'll say anything out their mouth to bring misery to somebody else", I replied as I reached in the refrigerator to pour me a glass of milk. Ashanti just watched to see if my whole demeanor would change in any way. But I had no reason to be jumping in my own skin because I was really telling the truth. You couldn't tell her that though. I could see it written all over her face.

"You just going to keep on with your breakfast like that bitch wasn't just on the phone with all that baby shit?" Ashanti said as she grilled me before storming out of the kitchen. I just sat there thinking dipping my pop tarts in my milk.

"I don't understand why any female would put herself through any type of embarrassment. Why she saying you're her baby daddy if you really aren't?" Ashanti shouted out again as she ran back in the kitchen like Evette from Baby Boy.

"I don't know damn, what the fuck! I just told you that shit isn't true. Let that shit go, leave it the fuck alone!" I finally snapped out on her which made her fall back as she could tell she was getting on my nerves. I left but let her know I would be back before she had to go to school.

I took off going to my Nana Lynn's house. It's the one place where I could always relax without worrying about anything. See my Nana Lynn was still technically my legal guardian and has raised me since the accident with my parents. I began feeling that I was too grown to live at home with her though. Ashanti's old lease was ending. We made the decision to start new in our own apartment. My Nana was all for it being that Ashanti has brought so much positivity in my life. She sees her really balancing everything out for me getting my life together.

"Hey Nana, I'm home." I said as walked into her bedroom. She sat on the edge of her couch that sat in front of her bed. That became her spot ever since my Pap-Pap past from Lung cancer. We believe it was from him smoking cigarettes like his life depended on it.

"Hey Baby, what brings you back over this way?" My grandmother smiled and asked as she was getting up to give me a hug and kiss.

"I just wanted to check up on you since I ain't been over in couple of days. You know, just making sure you don't need anything." I said.

"Boy stop, if there's anything that I need you know I'll go get it myself. Plus, I'm going out later. It's bingo night tonight." Nana replied. We both chuckled and conversed for like an hour. I sat there with her until it was time to go get Ashanti for school.

I pulled up to the house. Ashanti sat waiting on the porch steps for me to take her to school. We had to stop by the gas station first though. She hopped in and we rode up to the gas station.

"Put 40 in the tank babe" I said as I handed her the money. We both got out of the car. I stood next to the pump as she went toward the store.

"Hey gorgeous" said a voice as I turned and peeped the dude grab Ashanti by the hand.

"Excuse you, don't touch me please." Ashanti said as she pulled away from dude like he had a disease or something. She kept her stride going toward the store. He started to say something else to her.

"Yo, fall back cuz. She good." I said as he turned around facing toward me now looking to see who had cut him off.

"Fuck you and that bitch nigga." he said aggressively.

"Aye, bitch ass nigga, fuck you." I said while starting to walk toward him.

"You don't want no smoke." he said as he lifted his shirt showing me a black Glock 40 on his waist as Ashanti came running back in between us. He gripped it and pulled it out while biting his lip. He looked left and right before tucking it again since the gas station was crowded.

"Babe its cool come on. We'll just get gas somewhere else." she said as she tried to push me the other way trying to calm the situation.

"Yeah you better listen to yo bitch, go get that shit somewhere else pussy." the guy said as a grin slid across his face as if he had just won the battle.

"You right, you got it. I'll see you around." I said before we both got in the car. The little scene caused a few heads to turn. He had the upper hand. My joint was still in the car. Honestly, he could down me or her at any time so I didn't say much to where if I was him he would want to open fire on us.

We pulled up to the house and I told Ashanti to pack some clothes for the next few days. I wanted her to stay at her sister's house until I could address the situation my way. Don't get me wrong; I'm not no killer. To be honest with you, I have never hit anybody yet. But pulling a gun on me was something I wasn't going to allow to transpire without consequence. The fact he didn't even have the audacity to use it pissed me off the most. My Nana ain't raise no bitch and I ain't about to become one now so it is what it is!

## "Lexi Da Baddest Bitch"

"Hello" answered Lexi.

"What's good Lexi? Aye is Don-D still there? I called his phone but it's going straight to voicemail." I asked.

"Yeah, he in here playing with my son like he's his daddy or something. Why what's up? You don't ever call me. I guess you finally realizing I got that medicine you been missing." Lexi said to me which came in no shocking manner. She tries to throw me the pussy at me every chance she gets if Ashanti isn't around or paying attention.

"Lexi not now. Just tell him not to leave. Some shit just jumped off and I'm on my way over there as soon as I drop Ashanti off at school." I said.

"Okay baby." replied Lexi before hanging up the phone.

"Hey Don-D, something just went down. Sales said he'll be over as soon as he drop Ashanti off." Lexi called out while walking in the living room.

"Iight bet, good look. Look, all this time I keep trying and you ain't giving in to nothing. What's up? I'm trying to fuck?" Don-D said as he walked closer to Lexi.

"Nigga please, you still ain't ready for this grade A pussy. I'd fuck your whole world up. I mean to the point if you saw me with anybody else male or female you would be ready to kill yourself. Trust me I'm saving your life." Lexi said to him. She never denied the fact that she goes both ways.

"Bitch please you need to get your mind right and let me bust it wide open." Don-D said as they stood face to face.

"You ain't man enough yet for all of this boo-boo. You know I'm not a hoe or a cheap whore. You need to step your game up." Lexi said before walking away and heading into the bathroom to take a shower.

Lexi was the complete opposite from Ashanti personality-wise. Ashanti is the sweet, genuine, more stable one. On the other hand, Lexi's a gold digging, manipulative, queen bitch. She likes to be referred to as the baddest bitch in the game. Ashanti and Lexi really didn't get along too well. Lexi has always harbored jealousy toward Ashanti. Growing up she always believed Ashanti was their mother's favorite child.

Mrs. Tonya was their mom. Her husband Earl Jackson had died of cancer over 10 years ago. He moved his family up here from Lincolnton, North Carolina to work in the steel mill. His death forced her to struggle to get by. She suddenly had to begin feeding, clothing, and providing for 3 ladies all on her own. Her only source of income was a part-time housekeeping job.

She couldn't do too many other jobs since she was an 11th grade dropout. She had Ashanti at the age of 15. By the time she was 16, she was married to a man who was 12 years older than her. She never had time for anything while being a mother. She abruptly moved back to North Carolina last year to go live with her mother who was ill.

# NAME OF DA GAME

Both of her children made their own decisions to stay in Pittsburgh where they grew up at. Ashanti and their mom raise Lexi through the years. Neither one approved of the lifestyle she wanted for herself. Lexi just found her own self-motivation as she didn't want to struggle like her mother. She was adamant especially since no other relatives of theirs lived in the city. Lexi relied heavily on men who were big time drug dealers as a way out of the struggle. That's how she got pregnant with her son Malik 3 years ago.

She was fuckin with some up-and-coming drug dealer named Cornell "Coc" Thomas. He used to trap in a crack infested apartment complex up the way. One day the task force ran up in the building and he opened fire. They fired right back on him. He caught 6 bullets − one to the heart & 5 to the left lung. He died right there on the spot at the age of 22 years old. Their son Malik was only 3 months old.

Coc's mom had 45k stashed at her house after paying for the funeral. She gave it all to Lexi. A few weeks later she suffered a heart attack and died herself. Since the money came through, Lexi has had a passion for fashion. Wads of money would make her pussy wet and if you don't have much, you'd never even know what color bra she'd have on.

I know when Lexi sees me, she sees the best of both worlds. She really sees a chance to belittle her older sister by fuckin me and catching my dollar signs. I'm also a few years younger so she probably has it in her mind that she can mold me the way that she wants to. I won't fuck her or do any dirt close to where she could get a whiff of it to try to blackmail me one way or another.

"Sales ain't get here yet?" Lexi yelled out from the bathroom.

"No, he just hit me and said he'll be here in like 5 minutes." Don-D replied as he sat on the couch watching TV as Malik drifted asleep on his lap. Lexi came out of the bathroom wrapped in her towel and scurried down the hallway. She dipped into her room shutting the door behind her. She was careful not to send the wrong message to Don-D of any possibility of anything between them.

"Yo!" I said as I walked into Lexi's two-bedroom spacious apartment. I made sure to call out just in case. I didn't want to walk in on her privacy. She was infamous for letting me see what I didn't need to see.

"Bro I'm in the living room." Don-D replied while Lexi yelled from her bedroom.

"Hold up Sales, here I come." Lexi said.

"You got that look in your eyes bro. What's good?" Don-D asked as we dapped each other up. We both did a double take as Lexi came walking out of her bedroom with these pink booty shorts. They displayed her pussy print, and her booty cheeks were hanging out the bottom just bouncing. Her thick thighs were slightly rubbing up against each other. You could still see that gap where her pussy sat. Not to mention that her flawless high yellow skin with her 5'7' 160-pound frame. She has a flat stomach with some nice ass titties. The tight wife beater hugged her upper half. She's literally bad as fuck. She had in some Brazilian bundles that were flowing in every way. I almost forgot why I was mad or even there in the first place.

"So, what happened Sales? I see you came filled with frustration." Lexi said as she could see the look in my eye while she walked toward us just smiling and glowing.

"Oh yeah, bro some nigga just pulled out on me. He had the nerve to act like he was gone shoot me." I briefed him before I explained the whole situation on what occurred at the gas station and why I wanted Ashanti to stay over at Lexi's house.

"Okay Sales, this what I want y'all to do. After I get dressed, I'm going to take a trip over there by the gas station. Describe what he looks like and what he was wearing. I think I know who that was, but I'll go around and see what I can find out about him. That way you have the drop or even something to go off of." Lexi explained as she went back to her room to change her clothing. Ashanti called to check up on me. No matter what was going on she was always making sure I was safe.

Lexi came out after a few minutes in a dark blue power suit with cream stripes going down her jacket and skirt. She looked like one of Russell Simmons' secretaries over at Def Jam. "Damn Lil Momma" Don-D said as he looked amazed at what he seen. The transformation looked as if she was on Oprah's level instead of some big butt gold digging hood rat.

"What does he look like and what was he wearing so I know?" Lexi asked.

"He's brown skinned about 6'1", skinny with a goatee. He was wearing a white tee and a rose gold Jesus piece. His hair is dreaded up. He kind of look like a fake ass Snoop Dogg. I explained as I tried to give the best examples I could give.

"Ok, I'm about to head over that way. Just keep an eye on Malik for me y'all." Lexi said as she slipped on her 3-inch-high heels.

"Aye, don't you feel that might be a too much and intimidating for your average street nigga?" I asked as she just stood smiling and shaking her head at me.

"You got a lot to learn. First off it could be too much and intimidating but I want him to approach me as high class. I don't want to seem high maintenance like the average bitch out here. I set my standard level so high that whenever he gets the chance to meet me again, he'll be such a gentleman. It sets a different tone and sends a different charm. Most likely none of his boys will be around because of the sensitive side I'm going to encourage him to show. Don't worry about it I got my part just make sure you can handle your business. And handle my purse too nigga because this is costing you when it's over with!" Lexi said, as she made money gestures with her freshly done manicured nails.

"Come on Lexi you already know I got you after it's all said and done. You know we speak the same language girl." I responded.

"And that's money!" Lexi said to me before grabbing her Louis Vuitton bag and heading out the front door.

As she walked out the door Lexi got right into her black 01' Escalade Ext that was sitting on factory rims and pulled off. The short drive only took 10 minutes to get from Wilkinsburg back over to the Highland Park area. She swung past the gas station and noticed he wasn't there.

She circled the block to a well-known back street named Sheridan Ave. This was an infamous spot for drug sales, shootings, parties, and robberies. That's the exact time he'd be on if he had any ties to this area at all. As she spun the bin and there, he was on the phone leaning up on a cherry red '95 Chevy Impala SS sitting on 24" Ashanti rims.

"Excuse me honey, I'm a little lost. I'm trying to find the gas station. I know it's on one of these streets. I just can't remember exactly where it is." Lexi explained as she pulled up on him. She made sure she was sounding sweet and helpless.

"Hold up, I'm going to call you back. Yeah love, you're close you just passed it up. But it's back that way on the main drag. Go down about two blocks." the man replied as he walked toward the truck. He was pointing back in the direction that she just came from.

"Awe honey, thank you so much. What's your name by the way?" Lexi asked sounding flirtatious.

"My name Tommy and may I ask your name?" he replied trying to sound all proper while reaching for a handshake.

"It's Latoya." she said as she shook his hand smiling all in his face. She was just flirting away.

"Let me ask you this. You look like you a real street nigga. You know, like you're about your business and all. What do everybody call you? I know you don't want people calling you Tommy all day?" Lexi asked and you could tell that it caught him off guard.

"I go by Tommy Gunz or just Gunz." he replied.

"Oh okay, well Mr. Gunz it was nice to meet you. Who knows? Maybe I'll see you around one day." Lexi said as she smiled while letting him look into her light green eyes once more.

"Hold up baby girl. What can I do to make sure that sexy smile always stays on your face and make sure I'm the one to make that happen?" Gunz asked as he continued to share and smile back into Lexi's eyes.

"That was cute, I think I might like that. If you give me your number, I'll call you and we can make further arrangements for that to take place." Lexi replied as she pulled out her cell phone to get his number. After getting his number and stopping past the gas station Lexi headed back home. She stopped past a family dollar and purchased a pre-paid phone which she plans only to use for Tommy Gunz.

"Aye I'm back" Lexi said as she entered the house.

"What's good Lexi, what you find out?" I asked, eager to know something about the guy that pulled a gun on me.

"His name is Tommy Gunz and he followed my whole routine. I'll be able to tell you a lot more about him after I activate the pre-paid phone. I met him over on Sheridan Avenue so most likely he's affiliated with them dudes over there. And before I forget, he was leaning on a cherry red '95 Impala SS with rims on it. Either it's his or it belongs to one of the dudes he hangs with." Lexi explained as she picked up her pre-paid and called customer service to activate the phone.

"His name is Gunz huh?" I said to myself as I sat there rubbing my chin hairs trying to remember if I ever heard of that name before. I immediately began calculating different ways to handle my problem with Gunz.

"Iight well this phone activated. I'll text him after I get out of these clothes just to give him this number. He gone hit me up after I get off work." Lexi informed me before sliding out of her heels and walking back to her bedroom.

"Don-D come here baby. I want you to go spin through there in your truck just to see if they still out on Sheridan Avenue. Call us and let us know when you get there." Lexi instructed.

"Matter fact bro after I do that, we have to go see Auntie. She should be about done. You go holla at the plug in the meantime and I'll meet you over at my spot so we can slide out together to Aunties." Don-D said as I agreed, and he left Lexi's house.

"Now Sales I want you to come to my room and listen while I make a call to this nigga" Lexi said continuing to make orders as she walked down the hall entering her room. She left the door open for me to follow behind her. As I walked in the room, I could smell the sweet scent of Juicy Couture™. I took a seat on her bed. She had black silk sheets on them. Swear I was sitting so comfortably. Lexi started to pull out another pair of booty shorts as she called Tommy Gunz and put him on speaker phone.

"Who dis?" Tommy Gunz said as he picked up his phone.

"Hey honey, how are you? This is Latoya. Are you busy right now?" Lexi asked as she undressed herself to her panties & bra set which was black.

"Naw I ain't busy. I'm chilling what's up beautiful?" Gunz responded.

"I'm okay just getting my things together for this board meeting I have. We're trying to merge with the National City branches in Pittsburgh. Next week I have to take a trip to NYC to make an exceeding proposal." Lexi lied as she was playing her role so perfectly. If I didn't know her like I did she would have me fooled too.

"Oh okay, that's good. I ain't going to beat around the bush so is it possible to see you sometime before you leave?" Gunz responded.

"Only if you can remember to call me after 5 o' clock when I get off work. Can you do that?" Lexi asked.

"Oh yea, I definitely can do that." Gunz replied before they said their farewells and rushed off the phone.

"So, what you think?" Lexi asked me, referring to their conversation.

"Yeah, that nigga biting heavy. Once you get him to where he thinks it's cool to be alone, I got him from there." I replied knowing in my mind that I wanted his head but didn't want to go to war. That's how shit gets hot. And when shit gets hot police of all sorts get to looking around the neighborhood and asking questions.

"Fuck that nigga! He's already getting what's coming to him he just doesn't know it yet. But I'm talking about me. I seen that look in your eyes earlier. Come on Sales, you know how the game goes. You take care of me, and I'll take care of you. Right about now I need some bomb dick in my life. It's been about 3 months. I know this pussy so tight, throbbing, and wet right now." Lexi said as she stood in front of me biting her bottom lip looking in my eyes waiting to see my next move.

I could tell she was serious. Hell, I did need her right now. I couldn't help but wonder if she would tell her sister. I just didn't want, nor could I afford for this situation to backfire on me ever. That's my girl's sister, I stood there thinking to myself.

"Yeah, you right" I said as I stood up and kicked my shoes off as my dick started to get rock hard in my sweatpants. I was turned on just looking at how beautiful Lexi is. I whipped my dick out as she caught my hint and got on her knees. She gripped my manhood and put it in her mouth. I dropped my pants to my ankles and stepped out of them.

"Oh shit" I said as she held me with both hands. She sucked and jerked me off while the spit from her mouth was all over. She made these sounds with her mouth like she was about to spit every time she went down. I liked to call it "that sloppy head."

"Uhmmmmm, this dick taste so good lay in the middle of the bed" Lexi said as she held it in her hands looking at me. I followed her order as I took my shirt off in the process.

I laid on my back in the middle of the bed as Lexi continued sucking my dick. Her head game was sloppy as hell. It wasn't long before my balls was soaked from saliva. She went in making all types of slurping noises. I pulled her panties down to her knees and slid just my middle finger in because the two fingers couldn't fit inside her. Her pussy was so tight and wet. She started to make moaning noises as I slowly crept my second finger in moving around searching for her spots.

"Come on, I'm ready to fuck." Lexi said. She sat up looking at me before getting up to grab a condom from her dresser. After sliding the condom on, she straddled over top of me with her back toward me and rode me like she was a Texas rodeo cowgirl.

"Fuck Sales, mmm," Lexi shouted as she bounced on top of my dick. She was smacking skin to skin every time she came down with much force. After a few minutes of that she showed signs of having an orgasm coming. She gripped her nails into my legs and slowly started to rotate. I grinded her hips into circular motions until she sat there just making faces.

"Owww daddy, I want you to give it to me like that. Please don't stop!" Lexi uttered out as her legs started to do the butterfly. After a few minutes she just sat on top of me smiling like she just won the lottery. She leaned over to the side as she told me to come here using her index finger. I pinned down her right leg with my left one then held her other one in the air as I thrusted my whole shaft into her. With every stroke putting a look of a helpless woman on her face. Her eyes got big like she had just seen something crazy. I started flexing her leg to her shoulder as I broke a sweat during our chemistry. She started to sink her nails into my arms.

"Come on, let me beat on this pussy from the back!" I said as I stood up wiping the sweat from my face with a towel. She followed my order as I pulled up behind her and put myself all the way inside. She let out a soft scream that sounded how Pinky does in those pornos. Once my feet were planted, I gripped her left shoulder & right thigh as I drilled her causing her to moan and scream as she gripped tight on the sheets on the bed.

"Fuck, oh my God, I'm about to cum daddy" Lexi shouted out after I was in it but a few minutes.

"I'm about to cum daddy fuck this good pussy." Lexi shouted out again as I started to cum and then it suddenly got super wet. I quickly pulled out and realized the condom broke. And in that same moment I had bust everywhere. It shot all the way up just missing her face and hitting her shoulder and hand.

#

## "Lies & Deception"

L exi ran to the bathroom she was trying her hardest to make sure it wasn't no cum left up inside. We both went ahead and showered and agreed to keep it between us. It was time to call Pimp for the next set of moves.

"What's up Unc? I need you." I said.

"Bet Neph, Spot C in an hour." Pimp said before he hung up the phone. That was perfect timing for me. I had just enough time to get a rental. I didn't want my car to keep being noticed. I needed to lay low and I didn't need anyone trying to clock my time shifts or whereabouts in the streets. If so, they could easily have the drop on me.

I called Mama Macy and she agreed to come get me a rental. I told her to meet me at my grandmother's house. I parked my car and put the tarp over my car so nobody would notice what was going on. We left out and trust me a ride with her always came with a talk.

"Aye thanks for coming thru on such short notice like this Momma Mase." I said as we walked out of the Enterprise with keys to a black Dodge Charger.

## NAME OF DA GAME

"It's no problem baby you know I just want you to be safe before anything. I don't know what I'd do if something happened to you or Don-D. Y'all my baby boys." Momma Macy said to me as she let out a pretty smile.

"We got 5 more years to hold strong before Big Sherm come back home. By then you two should be into your businesses comfortably. Don-D should be finishing up with college around that time. He should be either going to the league or landing a great job to where y'all will be set for life. Y'all are never to let my grandkids walk this side of the track. Never let these streets, money, or those fast ass bitches come between our family or what you and Ashanti got!" Momma Macy went in.

"Without family or a great woman as your backbone, you don't have anything baby. If anybody tell you different it's all lies and deception that will send everything you ever worked for and achieved down the drain. Just remember that. Since we first started this, it's changed so much. Ain't no code, loyalty, or honor in these streets anymore. Our technology is becoming so advanced which equals more access. The feds are just sitting back and plucking y'all out of the dirt like y'all worms. Keep the words that I always tell you close to your heart. I love you and I'll see you back at the house soon." Momma Macy explained to me.

She was always down to give me some wisdom from her point of view. I always listened too because she has been through so much. She gave me a hug and a kiss before I got in the whip pulling off heading to spot C which was his club.

Pulling up to Chocolate City in the daytime was always so busy. Vendors are constantly delivering liquor and food. Our cleaning crew is always there cleaning up from the night before. It's always hectic in the club but it's just daily operations. It's always wall-to-wall but ironically few have ever walked upstairs. Only a few have ever even been inside of Pimp's office. He has built up this wall of trust. It really ain't no such thing as trust in his eyes. Nobody ever comes close to him or his office door except me.

"What up Unc?" I said as I walked in his office. His door was already open, so I shut it behind me.

"Sit down Neph." Pimp said as he directed his finger toward the seat right across from his desk.

"Now you know money don't grow on trees, right?" Pimp said as I nodded my head in agreement.

"But pussy do Neph." Pimp said as he checked his phone. He always made sure that the battery was out when he talked up and up no codes. Batteries had to be out of phones, and I respected his mind. It was always safety first for longevity and everything else will come to you in due time.

"That's how you get the money Neph. I have to go out of town for some shit. I got to take care of some family issues. When I say family, I mean money. I'm going to leave you a whole bird to hold you over until I come back. Now don't go showboating on me. Keep the same profile. Keep everything the same until I get back. Now I'm only leaving all this with you because I think you will do right. You hear me? I said that I think. Go and meet them at Spot E but stop past A first and we'll talk money when I get back." Pimp directed & explained to me.

"Aight bet, and I got you Unc." I said before I got up out of my seat and walked back to my ride. I had to stop past my house to put this black Glock 19 in my ceiling. It's the type with the drop tiles like a classroom. This way if I'm pulled or being watched that is one less problem I'd have to worry about.

I stopped over Pimp's sister house but there was never anything there. It was time to get to business. I left and went to spot E which was the car wash on Butler St. It was inside the drive through garage which was perfect. I never had to get out of my car, and everything was stashed inside of my trunk. I had it duck taped, rubbed down with Vaseline and Saran wrapped in my mesh bag of dirty clothes.

That move was always a smooth process. I left and headed to Nana's house to store all the work I had on me. I stashed it at my grandma's house because it was so lowkey and completely out of the way. I went in through her back door and hauled the laundry bag in the house upstairs to the attic. I had a safe buried in the attic floor and I also had a mini fridge. It was unplugged but I would use it from time to time to store shit in. I popped open the laundry bag and took out 5 zips and stashed everything away before I left the house to pick up Don-D.

"What's up, we good bro?" Don-D asked as he got in the car.

"Yea I got 5 zips on me." I responded.

"Okay bro, man you wouldn't believe that I spent all night with Lexi and ain't pound nothing." Don-D said in a frustrated voice as I pulled off.

"Aye bro fuck that bitch she ain't wifey material anyways. Go fuck with some stable ass bitches. That bitch is shady as fuck. You see what position she's playing with us. Once you make it to the league it's gone be a million women like Lexi. I ain't trying to burn bad bread on her but I don't see her ever making it past where she at." I said talking shit on Lexi hoping to alter his mind to want to chase other bitches. I really did not want to tell him what just happened between us just a couple hours ago.

"Yea, you right bro, I got a night cap set up with these white bitches. They ready for us bro whenever we close the night off" Don-D said. He sat back and turned the Jeezy up as we cruised back to Auntie Michelle's spot back over in the towers.

"What's goodie Auntie?" I asked.

"Nothing, just keeping everything afloat around here what's up baby? What did y'all bring with y'all?" Auntie asked as Don-D tossed her the zip-lock bag with the chunk of 5 ounces of raw cocaine as you could see the crystal-like flakes on it.

"Now that's 5 right there, are we straight?" I asked as she signaled to the bedroom to go get the money from the shoebox. Don-D walked right back to the bedroom to retrieve the money.

"It's 7 g's here" Don-D shouted from the bedroom.

"Yeah, each one is rolled up in a grand a piece." auntie Michelle said.

"We cool now, thank you auntie. Bro gone go shopping for you to make sure your groceries is up to par later. What else do you need?" I asked.

"I'm okay, thank you baby. But y'all don't want to cook it?" asked auntie.

"No, we going to watch you work your magic today." Don-D replied as he stuffed all the money in a little book bag that we had left there before. I sat observing her as she whipped everything up. She brought back 6 ounces, and the scrape up equaled another quarter. We told her just like before we only wanted the 5 back and the rest was for her to pocket. Her shit was so pure, she had dry cooked it and could probably be finished in about 12 hours or less.

We left the apartment heading to drop Don-D off at Lexi's house along with the bread. I had to run and grab Ashanti from school. We rode back to her sister's crib so me and Don-D could count the bands.

"Over the next few weeks, we gone to have assign some new muthafuckas to start going to see Auntie. We also have to connect with a new fiend that can make it boom like her spot somewhere else just to be on the safe side." I explained to Don-D being that spot was doing way too good and it would only be a matter of time before shit hit the fan. Because truth of the matter is nothing this great last forever and you don't never put all your eggs in one basket either. We had to unbind each roll of money to make sure everything added up to 7gs. If not, we had a problem.

"Yeah, your right bro. I meant to tell you my cuz Trigga Tre' came home today. He beat the body since both witnesses changed their story multiple times. Every statement they gave seemed to be different from the earlier one. As you know without a witness the D.A ain't got shit." Don-D said as I nodded my head in agreement with his statement putting a smile on my face.

"I talked to him like an hour ago. He at his baby mama's spot fuckin her brains out. I told him we'll come scoop him up tomorrow. I plan to take him to the mall and shit to get him right. Honestly, I was thinking maybe we could get cuz to handle them niggas. You know he was down for his 3rd body. You know this is exactly what he lives for." Don-D explained, wanting me to see the plan he was thinking.

"Naw hold up cuz, to outthink a cop you must think like a cop. You know if his name been ringing about bodies they'll be watching him closely. On top of that, cuz got a seed. I'm gone handle this myself. You know he into so much and his dirt keep adding up. He pretty much looks like Public Enemy #1 right now." I said to Don-D as we both sat there momentarily just counting money until Ashanti & Lexi both came into the kitchen.

"Shawn we just ordered some pizza & wings. Whenever it gets here can you pay for it? We about to run to the store and go get some breakfast food and some other things that we need around here." Ashanti said.

"Iight how much y'all need?" I asked.

"Only like $100 and just in case I have $100 on me too." Ashanti said. I peeled off two crisp 50-dollar bills and handed them to her as she was leaving out of the kitchen. They grabbed little Malik and left the house.

"Is everything still on deck for tonight bro?" I asked Don-D referring to the snow bunnies he had in line.

"Ain't even no question bro." He responded as we finished counting the money. We had to band it up and put it into different bags. He got what was his and I put mine to the side.

"I'll get what you owe in a couple days' cause Pimp just gave me a whole thang to hang onto for consignment."

"Word? All yea, we set baby." Don-D screamed as he hopped out of his seat with a bunch of excitement. Nigga ended up knocking his chair over in the process.

"Come on bro let's move this shit. We can sell half zips for 500 and wholesale onions for 950 of that fish scale. We could even compress them and sell them for $800 each bro. We can move that by the end of tonight. Come on bro, what are we waiting on? We're counting this money and we got money to clock." Don-D said to me. He became anxious immediately after I told him what Pimp left with me.

"Chill, chill, chill." I said, trying to de-hype the situation before I broke everything down to him.

"He went out of town for a few days. This is all we got to hold us over until he comes back." I explained to him.

"Well, when is he coming back?" he asked me.

"I don't know bro so we can't change up our status right now. On top of that, we have to get this retail money while we still can. Fuck that wholesale shit. We'll lose so much money and be way more of a target for jack boys & the cops. The streets talk like females these days."

Listening to stories from back in the 90's, it's nothing like it is today. Not just anybody could post up and hustle nor could niggas just wear whatever they wanted to wear. I'm talking down to rocking braids. Shit that's why it's so many rats now. Niggas ain't built for the streets. They jump out here thinking they're built like that. Shit niggas ain't never seen "Paid 'N' Full." I explained to him. He had this disappointed look on his face like I just let him down or something.

"Iight so where you want to put it at?" Don-D asked

"I already put it up. We'll just nibble on it when it's time to. It's just like we going to re-up because we still have to put this money up. He fronted this to us. We have to do this right. You feel me?" I said to put him up on game so he could calm his excitement.

"Iight cool" Don-D responded.

"Yeah baby, our birthdays are in two days. Are you ready?" I said trying to change this subject to something more positive for us.

"I can't wait! We gone do it big bro. We gotta be fly as hell." Don-D said eagerly.

"Hell yeah, it's our day." I responded.

"Go head and drop your bag off then come back and get me. I want to get some hotel rooms out this way just in case plus I have to get the food." I said as Don-D gave me this smirk then I continued. "And I just want to be here when my girl gets back nigga so what." I said as I ran out of excuses. We both broke out laughing at me and how I acted once it came to Ashanti.

"Aww nigga you wild." Don-D said to me laughing before shaking my hand then took off out of Lexi's house to go get the room with his fake ID leaving me there alone.

I barely trust Lexi so I'm playing her close toward all situations and all angles. I'm just trying to play the game how it goes. She honestly got everything in her hands to either make or break me.

"Is y'all still at the house?" a call came through on my cell phone from Lexi.

"Yea, y'all on y'all way back?" I asked.

"Yea we'll be there in like 5 minutes." She said.

"Did he call you yet?" I asked looking at the time noticing it was a quarter past 6 o'clock.

"Yeah, he did. I'll talk to you in a minute when I get there." Lexi said to me. I sat there just relaxing for a few minutes before she came walking in the house.

"What up doe?" I said as Lexi entered the crib by herself.

"Where are they going?" I asked as I seen Lexi's truck pull off again from out the window.

"She's going back to the salon to get her nails done. Her nail broke and Malik cried & begged to stay with her. They should be back around 8 o'clock." Lexi said as she took off her flip flops and sat on the arm rest of the couch next to me.

"Hurry up and call your girl so I can call him." Lexi said all nonchalantly.

"Naw she cool. I'm just going to put my phone on vibrate. This way if it's important I ain't missing much." I replied while waiting on Lexi to call Gunz. I could tell she was thinking differently as she smiled and pulled out her pre-paid and called him.

"What's up baby girl?" Gunz said as he picked up the phone on the third ring.

"Hey, how are you?" Lexi replied in such a sweet voice.

"I'm chillin, just trying to stay out the heat until it cools down some more." Gunz replied referring to the hot August day.

"I feel you on that. I was in the shop earlier getting my nails done when you called. That's why I told you I'd call you right back. What's your plans for the rest of the evening?" Lexi asked him.

"Shit chillin probably going to a bar for a couple of drinks. Why what's up, can you join?" Gunz asked as Lexi rolled her eyes and smiled.

"Oh no, I'm not really a big drinker but I do smoke on occasions though." Lexi said lying to him making it seem like she a goodie. Truth be told, she has her own bar in her kitchen. She keeps it stocked and she smokes by the pound.

"Oh yeah?" Gunz replied.

"Yeah, plus I have to work tomorrow. We can do lunch if you don't mind coming downtown around noon." Lexi asked.

"Yeah, I can make that happen." Gunz replied.

"Cool, well text me babe. I'm going to wash clothes and take a hot bubble bath. I need my body to relax for the night." Lexi said teasingly.

"Oh yeah, well you do that lil mama and I'll holla at you later." Gunz said to Lexi before hanging up.

"You got company coming over?" I asked as I got up and peeked out the window to see who it was. I gripped my 40 from up under my shirt.

"Oh, it's the pizza boy." I said as I seen the Pizza Hut sign on the side of the car door. I put my gun away and then opened the door.

"What they just now making it here? She asked me.

"Damn what took y'all so long?" Lexi said snapping as she answered the door.

"Hold up my apologies. It's my first day and I don't know this area too well." he replied.

"Well how are you going to take…" Lexi started to snap again before I cut her off this time.

"Lexi come on, chill girl. My fault man how much is the food?" I asked as I peeled a few bills out of my pocket. I keep my small bills on the outside and the big bills on the inside.

"$24.60 sir" he replied.

"Here goes $30, keep the change" I told him/ He handed Lexi the food as I handed him the money.

"Thanks, I appreciate it very much. By the way, y'all look good together." the pizza delivery boy said before heading back.

"But we…" I started to say before Lexi cut me off.

"Thank you that was so sweet of you to say." Lexi was blushing and smiling at me as we went back in the house. I shut the door and walked over to my phone to check and see where Don-D was at.

"What's up bro?" Don-D said as he picked up his phone.

"Where you at? Are you good?" I asked.

"Yeah, I just left the spot. Now I'm on my way to go grocery shopping for Auntie right quick. I'll be back in like an hour." Don-D said. Lexi could hear him speaking because my squawky was loud. She started smiling at me. We said our farewells and hung up the phone.

"Come on Sales, give me that daddy dick one more time." Lexi said as she stood up smiling rubbing her hands along my chest.

"You nasty as hell girl", I said as I just sat shaking my head as my dick quickly got hard. Her sex appeal and her aggression turned me right on, I can't even lie. I stood up locking eyes with her. She pushed me back down on the couch and then she reached for the remote. She hit play as she slowly started to undress herself to the words.

"Sales, lay it on me, I place no one above thee." Lexi sang the R Kelly song as she slow wined in front of me like she was Shakira showing me the perfection of her red bone body. I quickly slid my pants, shirt & boxers off leaving my dick poking up. She bent over gripping my dick shaft as she let the spit roll off her tongue onto my dick. She started deep throating. Lexi bobbed up and down while playing with my balls. She was giving the best head she gave me thus far and it was about to make me cum quick as hell.

"Oh shit, I'm about to nut." I said as I just sat back watching Lexi continue to go up & and down. She picked up speed while she looked in my eyes until I busted into her mouth. She kept on going and I grabbed the back of her head guiding her up and down so she knew to continue. She had my mind going insane. When she finally stopped, she looked up at me and opened her mouth to show me she swallowed it all. She went back down and started sucking again. She was slurping and making all types of noises. It's like she alternated between sucking me off and stroking my dick with her hands. She put my balls in her mouth and kept sucking on them adding to rotation as well. After about 5 minutes, she stood up then bent over beside me.

"Come on, there is a magnum in my purse." said Lexi. I retrieved it and slid it on before shoving her face in the cushions. I gripped her thighs tight. All you heard was loud smacking sounds of her ass slamming into my body. She was loving that rough shit.

"Oh my God, give it to me daddy." Lexi muttered out as I continued to plow away on her for like 20 minutes straight before busting again. I was going in and sweat dripped down my body as I came to a halt. Right then her body collapsed, and she rolled off the couch to the floor.

"Okay you made your point. My head hurt now come on we have to stop. I got the point that you about your business, you and that dick dangerous" Lexi said as she sat on the carpet rubbing her forehead looking up at me. She looked like she was on cloud 9. I gave back a quick smile before I headed to the bathroom and started cleaning myself off. I stood there in nothing but my socks. When I finished up Lexi came in and got herself together. She lit some incense to get rid of the smell of sex that filled the air.

After that I grabbed a couple slices of pizza. Me and Lexi sat on the couch watching TV. A few minutes passed and Lexi got up to unlock the door for Don-D. He came in the crib looking confused because we were in the house alone and sitting close as hell to each other. I could tell he noticed how close our plates were on the table and everything. Lexi walked off to the bathroom after she locked the door behind Don-D.

"Yo, what's up with y'all?" Don-D asked.

"Shit waiting on you." I said shrugging my shoulders as I answered his question. He shrugged his too as if he was dropping the subject. He walked off to the kitchen and Lexi followed behind him.

"Beep beep" my squawky went off again as I didn't recognize the number.

"Who is this?" I said as I squawked in.

"Dis Trigga Tre' what's up whoadie?" he answered.

"What's cracking nigga? Welcome home, you good?" I replied.

"Yea I'm chillin, I'm just balls deep in some pussy. Feeling good to be home and up out that bitch." Trigga Tre said referring to the county jail.

"Yeah, I can dig it. We gone link up real soon." I said.

"Yeah, that's cool. What's up with breakfast in the morning? I need to rap to you about a few things." Trigga Tre said.

"Yeah, I can fuck with that. Breakfast at Eat N' Park 10:30 then from there we gone get you fly. Our birthday coming up in a few days you ready for it?" I asked.

"I know it's on the 29th. What's the game plan?" asked Tre.

"I'll let you know. Don't make any plans either because we gone do it big. This really gone be a time to remember." I informed him while we chopped it up for a minute before ending the call.

"What's good Babe?" I said as Ashanti came walking in the house with little Malik.

"Hey baby, what's up with y'all?" Ashanti said as she walked over to me giving me a kiss then flopping down next to me seeming exhausted.

"You tired?" I asked her after she let out a big sigh.

"Yeah, I am, I just want to relax and get some rest." she replied.

"Well come on let me take care of you." I said before I got up off the couch. I grabbed her hand and led her to the bathroom.

# NAME OF DA GAME

She stood there smiling as I started to run her bubble bath. I lit candles and placed them around the bathtub while she waited.

"Aww this is so sweet baby" Ashanti said.

"You know it ain't about nothing babe. Anything to make you happy. When we first met you smiled so the aim has been to keep it up there." I whispered in Ashanti's ear as I started to undress her kissing her on her neck passionately.

"Aww babe don't ever change. I love you so much." Ashanti said to me before we kissed passionately waiting as the tub filled up.

"Come on, get in." I said as I leaned over to stop the water. She submerged herself in the tub. I stood watching, admiring her beauty. After a while, I grabbed her loofa and passionately washed her body from head to toe. I had to have a moment with my baby before me and Don-D headed back out of the house. We had some plans to tend to.

"Aye the room is already paid for. We just have to slide past the spot and get some coke. You know they snort that blow. We also need to hit Wines & Spirits to get a bottle before we go and pick these hoes up." Don-D informed as I sat back in the passenger seat.

"Where we going to grab some coke?" Don-D asked as we stopped at a red light.

"Slide past my Nana's spot." I responded. We cruised over to my grandmother's house. I wanted to ask him was we taking fiends to the hotel or was they just a few party bitches. I just let it go because its Don-D and party bitches is his type.

"Wait right here I'll be in and out right quick." I said as I got out of the car heading to the house. All the lights were on including the porch lights. More likely than not this meant my Nana had left. Nine times out of ten she was at bingo with Ms. Wilma. That's her neighbor from across the street. I ran up to the attic and eye balled a ballie on the stingy side. I bagged it up and headed back out to the ride. Now it was time to get fresh & grab a bottle for the night.

"Come on, let's stop at the liquor store over by my crib. I need to grab a few things for tomorrow". I said as Don-D had already gotten situated. He had changed his whole lay and had Louis his Vuitton duffle bag in the back seat.

"Iight bet we out then." Don-D said as we took off heading back towards my crib. We pulled up to the liquor store and caught a man coming out. I handed him three twenty-dollar bills and asked him to grab me a bottle of Grey Goose. I told him to keep the change. He came out a few minutes later with the bottle in the clutch and we went about our night.

"Sales check it out bro. Ain't that the ride Lexi was telling us about? A red Impala SS with rims, right?" Don-D asked.

"Yeah, that's exactly what she described." as we watched the car pull up to the opposite side of the street at the red light.

"He got his turn signal on so they're headed up the hill right here. We gone wait a few seconds and let some cars get in front of us. Then we gone slide up and see where they are going and who's all in the whip." I said as Don-D waited for some more cars to turn up the hill.

We then blended in traffic to see the destination of the car. As we hit the bin they parked, and three men jumped out. They were looking all around and walking up on a porch. We drove past as I took a good look at them.

"See Gunz is the nigga with the Plaxico jersey on. The short one is B-Nasty. He used to come down to the YMCA when Kayla use to work there. As far as I can remember he was quiet and reserved. You already know it's the quiet ones you have to watch out for the most. Come on we out bro. Now their spot has been exposed and we'll definitely be back." I told him.

# NAME OF DA GAME

"Why don't we just post there right now? We should just wait for them to come outside and let the choppas do all the talking from there." Don-D suggested.

"Naw bro, we don't know what's behind door number 1. That could be their arsenal crib. Or it could be like 12 niggas up in there probably all smacked down. Always keep in mind, it's chess not checkers. We got too much to lose. Look there's two cameras on that building right there too." I said trying to get Don-D to think more sharply.

"Yeah, you right bro. But what if that's a bitch's spot? It's late night now bro every street nigga trying to lay up in something or at least get his dick wet. Unless he trying to get back some money and time. Shit just think, where we on our way to?" Don-D asked me as we pulled up to my crib.

I went in and picked out a fit for tonight and one to wear for tomorrow. I grabbed my Louis Vuitton duffle and got everything together. I made sure I had my Glock with two extra clips and the slugs that had already been wiped off. The only reason to have them is to use them. I planned on using it when needed. I hopped in the shower and got dressed. It was time to go and enjoy the night. I threw my bag in the trunk because if we got pulled over everything would be back there. If for any reason we were pulled over, they'll have no reason to search because we have our driver's licenses.

"Where are we picking them up at?" I asked.

"They right along the way in Fox Chapel. They gone follow behind us. I called them while you were in the shower and told them we had shit to do in the morning. They just gone drive themselves" Don-D said just as Ashanti started calling my phone.

"What's up baby girl?" I said as I picked up the phone before I decided to turn down the music so she could hear we were in the car.

"What are you doing babe?" Ashanti asked.

"On the highway. We're on our way to Ohio right quick to go handle some business. Then coming back to the city to get ready for shit in the morning. Are you okay?" I replied.

"I'm okay I was just checking on you. Just making sure you're good. I ain't gone waste your battery but make sure you call me whenever you get there. I want to make sure you made it safely."

"Aight I will babe thanks for the checkup." I said before hanging up the phone.

"Okay Suave" Don-D said jokingly before I turned up Jeezy again.

"There they are in the Benz over there." Don-D said as he got on the phone telling them to follow us as we pulled up to the light. They hopped in traffic right behind us.

"You found some rich bitches. How you meet them bro?" I asked.

"I was at Victoria's Secret looking for some perfumes for my mom. They work there so you know I had to see what they about. And here we are." Don-D said.

"Okay I can dig it. You know I still brought my gun. I don't trust them still." I informed him.

"Fuck it I don't trust them either." Don-D replied as we pulled up to the Comfort Inn. We got out and introduced ourselves as we grabbed our bags.

"Aye Sarah, Chrissy this is my brother Sales. Sales this is Sarah and her best friend Chrissy." Don-D said as I greeted both with hugs.

"Your brother is real handsome Don-D." Chrissy said as she stood 5'3 with blonde hair, blue eyes. She was well put together. From head to toe she was gorgeous.

"Thank you and you're drop dead beautiful." I replied as she started blushing which made me smile a little. I was just trying to break the ice as we all walked inside the hotel. Once we got into our room, we got situated and made ourselves comfortable.

"Aight look bro, I like to sleep in the bed closet to the door." I said to Don-D.

"Ain't gone be no sleeping tonight so you can save those thoughts for a different night baby." Sarah said as she looked at me smiling with her perfect white smile. She had brown eyes and silky black hair that came down to her shoulder blades. She had a skinny build like Chrissy but just taller.

"I hope you can hang then." Don-D said to Sarah.

"Question is can y'all hang? We came prepared for what tonight may bring." Chrissy said with some humor.

"Y'all gone need more than your Wheaties breakfast & daily vitamins to hang with us for real." I said sarcastically.

"And y'all gone need Lil Jon's Crunk juice and Red Bulls." Chrissy said, giving me the same sarcasm back as we all broke out laughing. I put the music videos on tv while Chrissy and Sarah went to go take a shower.

It was perfect timing just as Ashanti had just called in to see if I had made it. I told her I ain't get around to calling her yet, but I was cool. I assured her I'd see her in the morning. I rolled up a stoagie of some purple haze and started facing until they came out and joined me. Don-D doesn't smoke or turn up, so it was just us three enjoying the bud. He made sure he put the towel under the door for us though.

"So, what's up? Do y'all dance?" I asked as me and Don-D helped ourselves to some Goose & cranberry juice.

"Yeah, you'll see when a good song comes on." Chrissy responded before I tossed them the ballie of coke.

"Now that ain't been really stepped on so be careful. It's the candy that'll make your nose bleed." I informed as Sarah rubbed it into her gums first to check the quality. Then they both poured the coke onto the nightstand and made lines. She pressed and chopped it down with her ID. They both took a turn snorting through a rolled up $20 bill.

"Wow this stuff is pure as fuck! Like the best I've ever had." Sarah said as you could tell her high was kicking in. She immediately started to dance to Pete Pablo's Freak-A-Leak song while so off beat. She bent over shaking her ass as me and Don-D sat on opposite beds facing the middle of the room. They both stood in between the beds as they stripped. They danced on each other until they both were completely naked. Chrissy then sat in my lap grinding before she guided my left hand to her shaved clit. She wanted me to feel all her juices flowing. I looked up to see Sarah bent over shaking her ass in front of Don-D. She focused back on Chrissy as she made sweet moans in my ear while I gently rubbed her clit.

"Let me snort and lick some coke off your cock. I promise you'll love it" Chrissy whispered in my ear as I signaled it was okay for her to do so. She got up and went and grabbed some using her ID on the nightstand. I leaned back on the bed while she took my shoes & pants off me.

"Oh my God!" Chrissy blurted out as she dropped my boxers and my dick stood at full attention. I laughed because she was really shocked at how my dick popped out. I stood there as she popped a pile on my shaft from her ID and then used the bill to snort it up.

"Sales don't hurt my best friend over there." Sarah said, joking as she could just sense what her friend's reaction was for. Chrissy then sprinkled drops of coke on the head of my dick as she twirled her tongue around licking it all off. My dick went numb in the process. She did it once more before sucking on my dick. She satisfied me with a decent blow job. She kept trying to deep throat and swallow me whole. She kept on pausing for a few seconds and

I'd literally feel my dick in her throat. She was a beast with the shit, kind of dry but she was choking on the dick. I ain't gone lie.

She then handed me a condom to put on while she put some more coke on her pinky fingernail. She took two quick sniffs before she climbed over top of my dick rubbing it on her pussy. She slid it in as she started bouncing on it halfway. That didn't do shit for me. I joined in and started fucking her back. I was slamming into her as she started to scream loudly. I made her take all this dick by holding her hips while she went up and down. She jumped off me and stood next to the bed holding her lower stomach.

"You cool? What's wrong?" I asked.

"I couldn't take it." Chrissy said as her face was turning red which made me smile as she stroked my ego which was already big.

"I got you. Get on all fours and arch your back." I instructed her. She did as I said, and I got behind her. She squealed as I went in before I started to pound her out. She put her face in the pillow and started screaming. That made me go even harder on her. I slapped her ass and held my forearm in the middle of her back. I watched her grip the pillow as I could hear Sarah screaming on the other side of the room.

I could see the veins popping out of Chrissy arms and forehead as her body collapsed. I started climbing on her body like Bunz did Keisha in Belly. I stopped after I busted my nut. I watched her body drop on the bed gasping for air. I stood up looking at my work before I went to the bathroom. I grabbed a rag and started the shower. Sarah came walking into the bathroom and shut the door behind her.

"I told you not to hurt my friend." Sarah said as she twirled her hair around her finger like I seen the white girls do in Sex in the City.

"What you want do then?" I said smirking at her before she snatched the rag out of my hand. She soaped up the rag up and took the liberty of washing and rinsing my dick off. She placed a towel down and got on her knees and put me in her mouth. She played with my balls with her free hand. She teased me by licking up and down my dick and sticking her tongue inside my pee hole. Her head started bobbing away again. She then stood up straight with a seductive look on her face as she walked past me. She hopped into the shower while I slowly stroked away on my dick.

She signaled for me to join her. I stepped right in, throwing my leg on the ledge to block the water stream in the shower for her She squatted down and deep throated as she twirled her hand and flicked her wrist. When it was time to bust, she let me cum all over her face. We finished up and showered so we could get back out of the bathroom. Chrissy was sound asleep in Don-D's arms.

"What's your story Sarah?" I asked curiously about the girl laying in the bed next to me.

"My story is simple honestly. My parents are both doctors and they are very wealthy. Their careers have them gone from home majority of the time. I spend a lot of my time with Chrissy. I'm also always working so I can learn to be independent before I go off to college next semester. I'll be attending Penn State to get my doctoral degree. What's your story? You got a name like Sales, that's so gangsta." Sarah asked trying to sound all ghetto and shit.

"Well, my story is simple. I'm chasing the money." I said keeping everything short and simple.

"Chasing money how do you like deal stuff, do you have heroin, cocaine, or meth, sorry I don't really know all the street names for that stuff?" Sarah asked me and I chuckled at first.

"Its dope, soft, ice, and I might. Why you ask tho?" I replied feeling like she ain't to be trusted.

"I know a few people that sniff blow but I know I bunch more people that shoot & sniff heroin." she said.

"I can probably get something the problem is trusting people to do business with." I replied expressing my concern to her.

# NAME OF DA GAME

"My brother and his friends get beat a lot. They either get robbed or they get some garbage. I mean occasionally they'll be satisfied but it's not consistent. Trust me, I wouldn't do this for any other reason. My schooling is already paid for. I just hate seeing my brother sick where he can't do anything, and they let it run their lives. I can you even pay you upfront that way you aren't taking too many risks with me. I can't even picture being in trouble. This is for you and my brother's benefit. You get some and he gets off sick and whatever else he feels. When he's well my whole family is happy and functioning but when he's sick it brings a dark cloud over us all," Sarah said looking me in my eyes. It all made sense to me.

"Okay we'll see what happens when I call you. I will say I do like your direct approach with confidence. That says a lot about your character. Look I'm tired and calling it a night. I have to get up early in the morning. Goodnight sweetheart." I said to her before I adjusted my pillow as she laid on my chest and we both went to sleep.

☐

## "Da Conversation"

## Aug 28, 2005

O h my gosh, we totally had so much fun with y'all last night. We have to do this again soon." Sarah said as we all finished gathering our things for check out time.

"We had fun too no doubt. We'll definitely keep in touch. We'll talk to y'all later. We're actually running a late for a meeting." I said as I gave them both hugs before exiting the room checking out. I hopped in the Charger waiting on Don-D as I looked at my watch. It was already 9:30 am and we still had to drive all the way across town. He came out and threw the bags in the trunk before we pulled off. We got there around 10 o'clock and Trigga Tre was already seated in a booth in the back. He had been there waiting for us.

"What's up cuz?" we both said at the same time. We had a lot of excitement seeing Trigga Tre finally home.

"What's smacking with y'all? Man, I been hearing great shit about y'all two." Trigga Tre' said.

"Yeah, like what?" I asked as we all sat down.

"Like y'all getting that money out here. And I heard Don-D the next Curtis Martin to come out of Taylor Allderdice High School." Trigga Tre said as he shook our hands again in joy for us.

"Yeah, so what's your game plan now that you're home?" I asked.

"I'm falling back cousin, I'm just paper chasing. That's it, everything else in the way. I really realized a lot being down there this time. Lesson number one is I ain't gone keep getting lucky beating these bodies. I'm also missing a lot of my son's life. This time around I realized I really am needed and loved out here. I ain't got shit to prove to anybody at all. I earned all the stripes I could earn already. I'm that nigga you feel me." Trigga Tre' said.

"Yea I respect it." Don-D informed.

"What's gone be your twist? What you trying to be fuckin with?" I asked.

"Well, the hard is home honestly. But once I see how niggas is moving and playing out here, I want to switch over to dope. Because ain't no money like dope money." Trigga Tre quoted.

"Yeah, what you know about that dope?" I asked. I wanted to know because I never touched it before – except as a middleman. I kept it around for a few of my snaps that did both boy and girl a lot.

"I used to cut and bag my ole head J Skullz shit up when I was younger in middle school. It was simple as hell. 10 bags in a bundle, 5 bundles in brick, and about gram and a half total per brick. It went for ten to thirty dollars a bag depending on where you at. I used to compare the coke hustle to the dope game with this nigga Gunz down at the county. He be trapping over by where you live at." Trigga Tre said.

"Gunz? You know that nigga?" Don-D asked before I could even say anything.

"Yeah cuz, we were on the same pod together until I went to the hole. Why? What y'all don't fuck with him or something?" Trigga Tre' asked.

"Naw, I just got into it with him a couple days ago." I spoke.

"Oh yeah? Fuck that nigga then. It's whatever and you know I'm booting up. What's up, what ya'll trynna do?" Trigga Tre' said as that devilish grin came across his face.

"We trying to get that nigga. He pulled a gun on me so he gotta see me ASAP." I said.

"What you know about him?" Don-D curiously asked as we all were leaning in closer.

"Well, I know that he was down the county fighting a body for like 2 ½ years. He be tender bout them bitches too, everyday that nigga sent mail out and twice as much if he ain't get none. He went to trial like a week before I did so he fresh home too. Everybody that was on that case trynna testify ended up dead fast as hell. I remember they was trynna say the last person was in a witness protection program and still got they issue but you know I don't know foreal but that's what the word was about it. His clique is called the Dope Boys. They for sure getting money because his books were flowing just like mine. Just like y'all dropped money on my shit, they did on his." Trigga Tre said as I started to rub my chin hairs.

"We gotta move fast and come up with something because he's a shooter too. I'm pretty sure he stays on point like we do." Trigga Tre said.

"We need to get him off his square. Honestly, what's a better way to do that besides pussy?" I said before I broke down what my plan was.

"Yeah, that could work but that is risky on her part." Trigga Tre said while we sat down eating our food. We finished up and headed off to the mall to go get Trigga's lays together.

NAME OF DA GAME

## "It's a Date"

## Aug 28, 2005

H ello" Lexi said as she answered the phone.

"What's up lil momma what time is your lunch break?" Gunz asked.

"Well for a second I thought you stood me up because it's already 11:30 and lunch is at 12 noon." Lexi spoke.

"Naw, I just finished getting ready I'll be downtown in like 10 minutes. I was making sure you didn't stand me up either." Gunz replied.

"Not at all honey. I'm still in my office going over some numbers for a meeting this afternoon." Lexi lied as she was downtown at Saks Fifth, shopping.

"Oh, okay so where we gone meet at?" Gunz asked.

"You can just meet me in the lobby at the big Citizen's Bank building in like 15 minutes. Then we can go from there. Is that good for you?" Lexi asked.

"Yeah, I'll be there." Gunz said before they hung up. Lexi hurried back to her Escalade to put her bags up and rushed over to the bank. She sat waiting for Gunz to come through the front entrance. He came walking in shortly after dressed to impress like he belonged there. He wore a cranberry Izod Polo, diamond pleated red straps watch, a pair of white Dickies shorts, and a pair of white Mauri's with a red & green stripe with no socks.

"Wow, you look beautiful." Gunz said as he embraced Lexi with a hug.

"Thank you, even though I'm in work clothes. You on the other hand are ready for the cover of GQ magazine, handsome." Lexi said flattering his dress game as he smiled back at her. They left the building and walked over to Mike & Toni's Gyro shop. They ordered the world-famous gyros and sat for a moment conversing. You know just getting to know each other.

"So Gunz, where you from?" Lexi sparked the questions off after ordering the world-famous gyros and fries.

"I'm from East Liberty. I grew up a few blocks away from where you met me at. What about you? Where you from beautiful?" Gunz asked, continuing to compliment.

"I'm from Cleveland, Ohio. I been here for almost a year. It's okay here but from time to time I miss home." Lexi said hoping he never seen her around before.

"What made you come to Pittsburgh in the first place?" Gunz curiously asked.

"I moved here for work. We needed to transfer a position down here and I came for the chance to experience a new city." Lexi answered.

"I can dig that. Get that money baby girl. Tell me what your last committed relationship was like?" Gunz asked.

"It's been two years since I had a serious boyfriend. He was a whore who didn't realize what I did for him. He was fuckin our whole neighborhood and even some high school kids. I just didn't want to deal with it anymore. He would put his hands on me from time to time when he couldn't control me. Eventually, I kicked his ass to the curb. The guys that came after him either didn't want much out of life or they swore they were big pimping.

For the last year I haven't even had sex because I just felt like it was time to focus on myself and my career. Whenever Mr. Right comes around, I'll know, and he'll deserve to enter my temple. My world is a like rare pearl and not everybody can have a pearl or even deserve one for that matter." Lexi explained, showing how quick on her toes she really was. She literally made all that up as she went along before asking him a question back.

"What was your last girlfriend like or are you a playa too?"

"Naw, I'm not a playa. I want to find Miss Right not Miss Right Now because life is so short. I want somebody to share it with." Gunz replied trying to sound all sincere.

"Are you for real or are just trying run game on me?" Lexi asked as she spotted the fly lines out in him.

"Naw I'm for real. To keep it real with you the last girl I had turned out to be a real smut. She was getting fucked by a bunch of people while I was locked up fighting my case. I found out she was a gold-digging ass bitch." Gunz said as he started to show some type of emotion toward his ex.

"I understand exactly what you mean now. I am going to keep it real with you. I'll tell you right now I like you and you're attractive. You seem bright, got all your teeth, and sincere. All that's left to find out is if you can make me laugh like you said you would." Lexi said seeing how vulnerable he was. Which made him smile.

"So how long were you down for?" Lexi asked.

"2 years" he replied back.

"What for?" she followed up.

"I was fighting a body that they mistakenly accused me of." Gunz said trying make it sound better.

"That's what's up. You beat it and got a second chance at life. What's your plans now?" she asked.

"I plan to get my GED then go to school for welding. I want to own my own welding company as well." he answered.

"Oh, okay that's a promising plan. So back to this ex-girl thing, do you still talk to her?" she shot back.

"Naw to be truthful I be disgusted when I see her out and about." Gunz answered while Lexi looked at her phone to see what time it was. She had to act like she was going to have to go back to work soon.

"What happened to the phone you had the other day?" Gunz asked as he took notice to a different phone. Lexi was smart enough to keep the other one in her truck.

"It fell in the toilet while I was fixing my hair. I had to go down to the Sprint store and get this one. I'm waiting for them to ship me a new one. I just can't not have a phone. I'd go crazy." Lexi said with a little humor.

"Oh okay." he replied. They sat and talked some more. On a serious note, they were having an enjoyable conversation. Lexi continued to tell the life of Latoya until her phone alarm went off. That meant that it was time to go back to work.

His phone went off during their walk back and she listened in on his conversation. He tried to code his words as best as he could. She could tell he was into illegal things though. He knew this moment might resurface with questions because she was all up in his mouth. She decided to hold her questions until next time they spent time together since this date went so well. He was just starting to open up to her. She didn't want to push it. Especially since they had plans to link back up after she got off work for a few drinks.

Lexi hung around in the women's lobby bathroom for a half hour. She waited until she thought the coast was clear. She figured Gunz would be out of the area by now. It's a fact that thugs and all types of gangstas don't really like to be out of their comfort zone. Mainly because they're more likely to be spotted by robbers or ones they were beefing with. Plus, the extra exposure was a sure way to get in trouble with the law.

Lexi made it back to her truck and she noticed she had two missed calls from D-Weez. She happily smiled and gave him a ring back.

"What it do Shawty?" D-Weez asked as he answered on the third ring.

"Hey baby, what's up? How are you?" Lexi replied sounding so seductive.

"I'll be in town tonight so get a telly. My plane lands in Pittsburgh at 10:30." He instructed as they talked for a few minutes before hanging up. Lexi hopped right onto it too. Whenever D-Weez came into town it was always most rewarding for her. She got dick, treatment of a queen and great conversations. He always gave her the best advice and left her with plenty of money.

See D-Weez was an up-and-coming rapper from East Atlanta. She met him on a trip down Atlanta at Club 112 during Nelly's birthday party. In da A he was somebody and had a lit ass crew beside him. He had her with him all night showing her off and treating her right. Then brought her back to 112 for a comedy show showing her a softer more intimate version of himself which swept her off her feet.

He's always doing a lot of touring and promo shit, so he stays on the go. But every chance he gets to come toward the East Coast he makes sure he spends time and money with her. He always gets her right until the next time he can see her.

With the sudden plans dropped on her she had to adjust and make everything go according to plan. She booked the Jacuzzi room at the Holiday Inn on the South Side. Then it was off to

# NAME OF DA GAME

Victoria Secret to get some sexy lingerie for a wonderful night with D-Weez.

She still had to get ready to see Gunz for drinks too. Before she did anything else she had to get it right, get it tight by soaking her body in a vinegar bath. She douched afterwards and showered before meeting Gunz at the bar.

She spent a while convincing him to come out from around his way and go to a white bar with her across town. The West Side is where she wanted to go. It was lowkey over there. She was there to execute a specific plan and didn't want people all in their faces. Her intent was to not have anyone watching their every move. If that was the case, she might not be able to do what she intended to do.

She left the house around 7pm. She had on a black dress shirt and a pair of jeans that hugged her so tight they looked like they had been painted on. She sported a gold Gucci belt and a pair of gold open toe 6-inch Gucci heels. She grabbed her black & gold Gucci purse and was ready to get the night underway. She hit Gunz with the directions to the bar.

Gunz arrived shortly after wearing green and white polo head to toe. They embraced each other with a hug and kiss on the cheek. They ordered drinks and went and sat at a small table opposite of the windows. He sat there slowly sipping his E&J as she did her orange juice. They conversed but she took it easy. Knowing she didn't want to be any type of drunk or smell like cigarette smoke she just chilled for the most part. She had plans to meet right with D-Weez when she left there.

She tried to get him to loosen up. However, she could sense that he was tense and uncomfortable. She went over to the jukebox and played a few hood songs like Snoop Dogg, Yo Gotti, Soulja Slim, and B. Gizzle. She even played some cuts from No Limit's C-Murder and Young Blood.

He started to feel more comfortable around her. During the whole two hours they were there Gunz never left the table. This enabled her to follow through with her plan. After a while it was time to end their date. She had to go take a quick shower so she could be ready for D-Weez when his plane lands.

# "Where you at boi?"

# Aug 28, 2005

I sat thinking how shit was blown out of proportion. I already knew that there was no changing Shawn's mind. He felt like his manhood was tested so no one was going to alter him from what he was going to do. I just pray that nothing happens to him. It was already bad enough that I worry about him coming home every night because he's out chasing money. Now he was trying to go gangsta. Everybody knows gangsta's only end up dead or in jail.

Now I look at my sister Lexi and I see how "Coc" dying changed her life for the worse. Her dreams had diminished after he passed. She became so cold-hearted and money hungry that it's all she ever talks about. It's to the point that I make sure that every day when I wake up, I refuse to be content with where my life is going. Especially when I just found out that I'm 6 weeks pregnant with Shawn's baby.

I've been scared to tell him because I don't know how he is going to take it. I hope when I do tell him he will be just as happy as me. I also hope that he will be willing to slow his life down. I know we can do this family thing together the right way. Matter fact there isn't even no point in keeping it away from him. I think I should give him a call and tell him now. He might rethink what he's doing now.

"What's up baby girl?" Sales said as he answered the phone on the 4th ring sounding out of breath.

"Where you at?" I asked curiously, wondering why he was breathing so hard. Ever since Kayla called his phone, that baby stuff been on my mind heavy. I wonder is he cheating on me? Like why would she put herself through all that bullshit if it were a lie?

"We all at the YMCA benching. I just got off when you started calling. Aye spot him for me while I rap to my wife right quick." Sales said talking in the background to his boys.

This always made her feel confident and more secure about her position when he addressed her to others with those types of titles. To her it was like him letting them know she wasn't alone at all, and he was there.

"It's cool Shawn finish your workout. When are you coming over to Lexi's house to spend time with me? I asked.

"I'll come and take a shower there. I have to drop Trigga Tre and his right hand, Gutta off. I'll be right over after that." Sales responded before hanging up and going about his business.

"I'm telling him today" is all I kept telling myself. I want to before everything gets too far out of hand. I feel he should know since he had Trigga Tre' around him and Gutta-Gutta aka Bad News too. That could only mean one thing. Shit was about to hit the fan soon, real soon." I sat and thought.

## "Let's Get it Cracking Then"

## Aug 28, 2005

D amn nigga, to be so skinny you sure get the weight up off you." I said talking to Gutta-Gutta. He was 21 years old, 5'10", light brown skin with braids in his hair.

"Yeah nigga, I'm strong as shit low key. I got major strength. It's just I be throwing back them beans daily." Gutta-Gutta said as he grinned showing his chipped tooth. We all joined in laughing and busting jokes on each other as we walked back to Don-D's Tahoe getting in and driving off.

"I got to get some gas right quick." Don-D said as we pulled into the Sunoco gas station.

"I'll get the gas. I killed my Gatorade and I'm still thirsty as hell right now. Do any of y'all want something?" I asked before I took their order and headed inside the store buying all types of snacks, drinks, and Swisher Sweets. As I was walking out of the store a cherry red Impala pulled up right behind Don-D's Tahoe. Me and Gunz locked eyes as he and his man's Biggie got out of the ride.

"Bitch made nigga!" Gunz yelled as he was walking quickly toward me. I did the same thing dropping the bag as he tried to square up with me. I had seen Biggie trying to creep around from the side.

"Thunn, thunn"

Gunshots went off as we both ducked and turned around seeing it was Gutta-Gutta who had a silver rubber grip 40 Cal. in his hand. He had just dropped Biggie as he squirmed on the floor right by the pump. Gutta-Gutta aimed at Gunz who took off running like Jessie Owens through the trees that was behind the Sunoco.

It was more shots that rang out and echoed by the gas station pumps. Trigga Tre, Don-D and Bad News were shooting in the direction that Gunz was running. We could still see his green polo shirt moving swiftly zig zagging through the trees.

"Fuck I missed and I don't ever miss. Come on Sales we got to go. Let that pussy nigga die slow." Gutta-Gutta said as I picked back up the bag and got in the ride. We took off flying down the street.

"Don-D slow down cuz, you gone get us knocked. Come on we going to my Baby Ma's spot on the Hill you know how to get there right?" Trigga Tre' asked as Don-D responded with a nod. We cruised over to Jamaya's apartment building on Bentley Drive.

"Jamaya where my son at?" Trigga Tre' asked as the four of us came barging through her front door.

"He's staying over my cousin's house tonight to play with her son." Jamaya responded as she sat up off the couch in his boxers and wife beater. Her eyes widened up as we all unconcealed our weapons.

"Oh my God Trayvon! What the fuck did y'all just do? You just came home yesterday. I swear you don't want to be in me and your son's life, you fuckin jailbird. You don't know how to chill not even a little bit. I swear I'm not doing no more bids with you."

# NAME OF DA GAME

Jamaya screamed before walking back to the bedroom and slamming the door.

Trigga Tre tossed his gun on the couch and stormed after her into the bedroom and slammed the door behind him. A few seconds later Trigga Tre yelled "Bitch" then right after that we heard Jamaya cry out "Tre get off of me, get the fuck off of me Tre. No, fuck you get off of me." Right before it all went quiet as we all just stood there listening for a second. None of us got involved in domestics on the strength that we didn't have a resolution.

If you get involved, you were the bad guy because you stuck your nosey ass in somebody else's business. I'm not trying to be captain save a hoe. This usually led to future problems with the male because he might feel you want his bitch. She might get mad because in the end you had nothing to do with it. On top of that couples make up 9 times out of 10. They work shit out after they get the shit bottled in off their chest. This is especially if they had time in together like how Jamaya and Trigga did. They been on and off since they were 14 years old. That's six years strong with a 3-year-old son.

"Come on lets clean our hands off. Their bleach is under the kitchen sink." Don-D said as he walked into the kitchen pulling out the bleach and handing it to me. We all stood over the sink as I poured bleach over their hands and wrist to get rid of any trace of gun powder residue they might have. As I looked into Don-D's eyes I could see he was nervous. Gutta-Gutta was paying attention too before he broke out laughing.

"You gone be cool lil cuz. I was the same way and that was like 8 years ago when I bust my first gun. You'll get used to it. You know I just get it how I live because its kill or be killed, you just getting ya feet wet that's all." Gutta-Gutta said with a little arrogance before we all walked back into the living room. We chilled smoking a blunt of White Widow as Gutta-Gutta told comical stories about bitches he was fucking.

Trigga Tre' came out the room in his boxers and socks sweating hard and breathing heavy. He came right to Gutta-Gutta just as he was sparking up the second blunt hopping right in our session. He dropped two blue dolphins on the table. Gutta-Gutta grabbed them to chew and suck on.

"Good looking Bro, she cool now?" Gutta-Gutta asked with a grin on his face.

"Yeah, she's happy again." Trigga Tre said being sarcastic which made all of us laugh.

"Fuck all y'all niggas!" Jamaya yelled from the bedroom which made all of us laugh even harder until my chirp went off.

"What's up Baby girl?" I asked.

"What's up, where you at?" Ashanti said in an aggravated tone.

"Some shit just popped off I'll be there later on." I replied.

"Shawn, Lexi is getting ready to leave she just got out the shower. Her sugar daddy from ATL up here for tonight so it's just me and Malik. I'm not gone be able to sleep until you get here so can you please be safe. Don't do nothing stupid and make your way over here."

"Aight, I got you. I'll let you know when I'm on my way." I responded before I placed my phone back in my pocket. Trigga Tre sat cracking jokes.

"Yeah bro, you need to make her happy now. Happiness gets results watch this." Trigga Tre said just as Jamaya came walking back into the living room and playfully smacked him in his arm. She came and sat down just smiling away.

"Bad News pass me that blunt." Jamaya said. He gave her the blunt and went back to being comical and telling his stories.

"Lexi, man that bitch a trip. I was trying to get the pussy the one day. She was all on my dick when I saw her at the after party a couple months ago. I looked up and she was all up in my VIP section. She even got her own bottle out of me. I usually don't even buy bitches drinks. I texted the fat bitch that work at the telly to have a room on deck. I'm thinking I'm about to beat it up honestly.

I popped two triple stacks and smoked a blunt of white widow with her. We sat chilling until it was time to leave. I asked her if she was going to ride with me or just follow me. I knew if she followed me we ain't got to come back out this way tomorrow. You know this bitch had the nerve to look me in my eyes and say okay but I need at least 3 stacks from you.

I looked at her and said bitch is you stupid? If anything, you should be paying me for this dope dick. That bitch had the nerve to say "give me…" one more time so I had to tell her like this "bitch my name is Gutta-Gutta. I don't give bitches shit but dope dick and headaches. Then I told her just like this – fuck you, get the fuck out of my face. I could have had another bitch or two by now with the bullshit."

I stopped her one more time just to make she sure understood that I wouldn't give her the satisfaction of me pissing on her tongue if it was on fire." Gutta-Gutta said as we all broke out laughing as I fell to the ground in tears before Trigga Tre put Don-D on blast.

"Aye Bad News, cuz been trying to hit for like a year now. Ask him what that money shot like." as Tre started tapping his baby mama's shoulder. Everybody could tell by the look on his face that Don-D didn't hit it. Which made everybody cry out laughing. Don-D was laughing too before Bad News shouted out "you should have paid the 3 stacks lil bro." as we kept the laughter going. We calmed down after a few minutes.

"Sales you know Kayla named her baby Shawn Rodgers Jr., right?" Jamaya said.

"That bitch crazy I ain't hit that in like over a year." I responded while shaking my head.

"That baby high yellow I seen it when she came home with him two weeks ago. Neither one of y'all is light skinned. Shit the baby's ears ain't even dark. You know that's some mystery shit when two black ass people make a bright baby." Jamaya said.

"I just keep that bitch away from me. She had the nerve to call me the other day trying to argue with Ashanti. She was talking all that bullshit about her baby being my child. Listen the last time we fucked was right over on that couch. The one that used to be up against the wall." I said as I pointed over to the wall by the door.

"That had to be over a year ago. I know because I had this new living room set for over a year now." Jamaya said as we all chopped it up some more. Gutta-Gutta was deciding who he was going to go fuck as he scrolled through his contacts. We all decided we were going to finish this shit off with these niggas. The worst thing that could happen is let this beef sit when we got family. One bad day could cause us to slip. That's just the nature of life.

We called Snipe's shop so we could store Don-D's Tahoe over there. We needed to get it painted too. There was no telling who seen what or who was running their mouths. We had to consider everything. If they had people looking for that ride that would be a sitting duck move. Trigga Tre and Don-D went to drop the Tahoe off and rode back in Tre's tan '94 Caprice Classic. I decided it was time to make my way to my girl for the night. I caught a ride with Gutta-Gutta to my rental then off I went.

Once pulling up I noticed Lexi's Escalade was already gone. Ashanti let me in the house quietly. We were trying to avoid waking up Malik. He was in his bedroom but also a light sleeper.

"Is everything okay Shawn?" Ashanti asked as I took my overnight bag into the bathroom after greeting her with a long hug and passionate kiss.

"Not right now but in a minute it will be." My response left a puzzled look on her face. She stood in the doorway of the bathroom trying to figure it out.

"Shawn what do you mean? That didn't make any sense." Ashanti asked again as I just ignored her and got into the shower.

I grew up watching hood movies along with the older niggas from around the way. I learned quick to never let a female know your business. Females work a lot differently than males.

## NAME OF DA GAME

Their minds were a lot easier to corrupt and they usually operate on emotions instead of morals. It's definitely the complete opposite for males.

Cops usually look for females to provide leads in cases because their favorite lines to them "he's going to let you go to jail for him that's not loyalty". The classic cracker jack threat is "we are going to take your kids away from you and you'll never see them again." That's when the maternal instincts kick in. Most of them start to break and give up information. To avoid the extra complications in my life I'd just keep what happens in the streets in the streets. It's not for her to know at all.

I'd rather not bring my secrets home that way she doesn't have extra stress. This would always prevent her from having anything to talk about. If shit ever hit the fan, they going to hit her with full court pressure. I'm not 100% sure that she can handle it. Now don't get me wrong I love her and trust her but only to a certain extent. Placing high standards on people and putting them on pedestal gives them a chance to fail you one way or another.

That's especially true the way the world is going now. Honor has lost its way. It ain't the same as it used to be. Back then, ratting was forbidden. You did stand up shit because you a man and knew what came with it and rolled ya dice as you may. Wasn't no such thing as all in until you got caught up with the wrong people or the law.

Ashanti joined me halfway through my shower. She pulled back the curtain and got in with me as we made love under the water. It was so sweet and sensual. Honestly just what I needed after all that had been going on. We finished up and got ourselves together. I fucked up her hair, so she had to pin it down for the night. We laid on the couch and fell asleep.

## "Chasing a Dream"

## Aug 28, 2005

H ey baby." Lexi said and gave D-Weez a long hug as he entered the hotel room. She had just hung up the phone from giving him the room number.

"What it do shawty?" D-Weez said as he sat his bag down getting a good glimpse at Lexi. She stood in front of him wearing a schoolgirl uniform that she bought from a sex store at the mall. She stopped there to get the red lingerie she was wearing up underneath.

"So how is it going career wise?" Lexi asked.

"Shit, everything going strong right now shawty. Last night I did the show in North Memphis with Yo Gotti. Today was travel time to get up to Youngstown, Ohio. I did my second show with the OHdime (oh10) niggas. When I leave here it's back down to Richmond, VA for a show I'm headlining. I wrap everything up in the A performing with Lil Jon and the Eastside Boys. I literally only have three days to rest while my manager put a deal in place with Universal Records. We're currently set on about 16 million.

Once everything is solidified, I'm heading to New Orleans and Baton Rouge. Last stops on this tour is H-Town and D-Town." D-Weez said with his face lighting up with excitement.

"That's so good. It's finally paying off. I'm so proud of you." Lexi said as she gave him another big hug. "Hold up shawty, you should be proud for us. Once I get this money up, I'm relocating you and your son with me to North or South Carolina. That way we ain't too far from either spot." D-Weez said referring to Atlanta and Pittsburgh.

In such a short time, Lexi became everything D-Weez had ever wanted in life. They meshed well from their compatibilities, conversations, and styles of swag. Their love for money and sensual love for each other was unmatched. She was the greatest wife ever to him and always made sure he was taken care of. She catered to him any and every chance she got.

He got shot in the chest one time in Miami. She flew herself and her son down to look after him. He had been hit in the arm and chest during a robbery attempt. He was on his way to a show in South Beach and shit went left. From that moment on, D-Weez always kept her close to his heart as his angel from up above. "Mr. Desmond Washington can you stop joking with me?" Lexi said trying to act like she didn't really hear what she just heard him say.

"Naw shawty I'm serious we chased this dream together. We out as soon as the ink hit the paper no bullshit shawty." D-Weez said as Lexi just jumped right into his arms. They kissed, touched, and caressed all over each other. They took that moment to really get caught up on lost time. He held her close while they relaxed and watched a movie.

They made love throughout the night all over the hotel room. He ate her asshole too for the first time. She gave him the best head and kept sucking after he bust. She climbed in his arms and fell right asleep when they finished. D-Weez knew he needed to go to sleep to try and regain himself for the days to come. □

NAME OF DA GAME

## "Business first, Birthday second"

## Aug 29, 2005

G ood morning baby, you look well rested." Ashanti said as she handed me a plate full of steak, cheese eggs, grits, and waffles. She sat a tall glass of strawberry milk down on the table. She kissed me and wished me a Happy Birthday. I quickly ate my food then went to the bathroom and cleaned up. I called Don-D to wake him up so we can get ready to make moves on our birthday.

"Shawn where are you going? It's your birthday. You don't want to just hang out for a lil? Let's catch a movie before we go out tonight to Chocolate City."

"Baby I got to take care of business first, then my birthday second. I'll be back in like 3 hours. Call me if you need anything, ok?" I said as I gave her a kiss on her forehead and walked out the door. I slid over to Don-D's mom's house. He had some bitches come stay the night with him. Momma Mace came out and met me as I pulled up. She walked out and sat in my passenger seat.

# NAME OF DA GAME

"What's up Momma Mace?" I said as I gave her a hug and a kiss on the cheek.

"I don't know you tell me." Momma Macy responded as she tried to read my poker face for some type of clue.

"What you mean?" I said playing the dumbfounded role.

"Well look I ain't trying to be in your business too much. But you are my business and so is my son. I don't know what's going on but last night I got so many signs that something wasn't right. When Don-D came into the house I tried to ask him a couple of questions. He did the same thing his dad does when he's lying to me. His right eye was twitching, and he became all defensive.

I looked outside and his truck wasn't here. I was watching Channel 11 news this morning and they said there were shots fired at the gas station. You know the one over by your house. They said they don't have any leads. There weren't any cameras by the gas pumps either. There was blood and shell casings from multiple guns. Police are looking to question the driver of a Tahoe." Momma Mace said before looking for a response from me as I just sat there motionless.

"They described Don's Tahoe. Now I have never worried about what y'all did because y'all was smart and lowkey. Y'all are my eyes in the streets. Y'all always gave me good reports. I have always seen the ambition in y'all eyes. I knew that this wasn't the end. It was just a stepping stone for both of y'all. Now I think y'all starting to get swallowed into this life.

Always remember the streets don't love nobody. If you die or go to jail God forbid but there will be some knucklehead to pick up where you left off. And it's always one to pick up where he left off and so on so forth. I don't mean to be preaching to you. But you are my son and Don-D is my son too. I carried him for 9 ½ months and pushed him out of this pussy. I don't want to lose all the men in my life. Y'all faces is what keep the feeling of Big Sherm so strong. I had the same gut feeling I had when Big Sherm started to deal with that new rat ass connect he had. I kept quiet because I always trusted and respected his intuition as a man. That caused me

5 years straight of lonely nights. Over and over, I fight the urge to move on with life. Since I was all in when it was good, I'm still all in while it's bad. Y'all got all y'all lives to live, have fun, and everything else. All I want y'all to do is slow down before it's too late. Money will always be around it's only paper." Momma said as she gave me a hug and kiss on my cheek. We got out the car and headed into the house together.

"Bro what's up?" We embraced each other with a handshake as I looked over and seen Nikki.

"What's up girl? You don't know nobody now?" I said as I gave her a hug.

"How you been stranger? You still be talking to my best friend Ashley, right?" Nikki asked.

"Naw not really but we still cool though." I responded. Just then I remembered that I had fucked her and then was fucking her best friend too. Then that one time I had her and her best friend going crazy fucking them and putting X and their bootyholes.

"Oh okay" she replied before walking out the door after saying goodbye to Momma Mace and Nevaeh.

"That girl nasty as hell." Momma Mace said.

"Huh?" we both responded as we turned to hear what she said again.

"That lil girl nasty, first you fuckin her, then he fuckin her. I hope she don't think I forgot her from before. Y'all better be careful because y'all just as nasty as she is. Y'all dicks gone fall off one day if y'all keep playing around." Momma Mace said.

"Ain't no fun if the homies can't have none." I responded as me and Don-D chuckled giving each other a pound.

"Okay 2-Live Crew enjoy y'all birthday and Sales remember what I told you. Take heed and talk some sense into Batman and Robin. Now leave the bat cave and lock the door behind y'all." Momma Mace instructed.

# NAME OF DA GAME

We dropped Nikki off and headed to my Nana's house to go get some work for Auntie Michelle. I squawked Sarah back and forth as we talked about her buying 4 bricks of them flame bags. She about to grab them for $600 each from me. I was also fronting her a half ounce of girl just to see how it move with her in control then I'll take it from there.

I had just called Gutta-Gutta to get her bricks for $200 each. This already puts me at a profit of $1600 just by middle manning a transaction. I went and grabbed 7 ounces from my Nana's attic. Then I took off heading toward Auntie's apartment in the Carnegie Towers. I hit Don-D because I still needed to talk to him about last night. I wanted to see where his mental was. The last thing I really want is for him to be is all in and say fuck his career.

"You know that shit made the news last night, right?" I asked as I turned down the music.

"Huh? Naw man I ain't even get a chance to watch it. What they say?" Don-D asked sounding a little shaking up.

"Dude ain't even dead. As a matter of fact, they don't even know who anybody was. They just said there were reports of shots fired. It was 35 shell casings collected but no reports of anyone going to the hospital. They are looking for a white truck owner for questioning." I informed.

"I took it to Snipes. He detailed it and painted it hunter green. It should be ready to drive again in a few days. I just hope ain't nobody running their mouth like bitches or I'mma dead they ass." Don-D said as he pulled a bag of purple haze and a blunt that I didn't realize he had behind his ear. He tried to light it up as I stopped him knowing that's probable cause to search the ride. I sprayed the air freshener to get the little bit of smell out. It was at that very moment I noticed something totally different about Don-D. His vibe told me he was all in now. He was for sure down for all the bullshit that came with it.

"Aye call Auntie and let her know we outside." I said as we pulled into her parking lot. We sat there shadowing things for a hot minute before I made my way to Auntie's apartment. Don-D came up 5 minutes later.

"What's up Auntie?" I asked.

"Nothing much but y'all missed about $400 taking so long. Shit some of them had so much money I had to go in my personal stash and break them off. That way don't nobody else get that money." Auntie Michelle said.

"Besides that. How's everything else going?" I asked wondering if any funny shit been twerking or money slowing? You know anything outside of the usual.

"Naw everything still everything. Not unless you want to hear about my sex life. You want to hear about that Kevin?" Auntie said showing a lil sarcasm.

"Naw, I'm cool. I got enough porno scenes in my own life already." I replied.

"I bet you do, you're a nasty mothafucka." she replied before we all walked into the kitchen laughing. It was time to take care of business and get to whipping shit up. I prepared everything while Don-D broke down the chunks of coke on the newspaper. He was on the kitchen floor using an old glass jelly jar and taps from the flat side of the hammer.

We weighed up and 6.5 ounces is what I cooked. We ended up with 8 ounces of straight drop hard after it dried up on the bounty paper towel.

I sent Don-D to the bedroom to grab the money once we finished up. Then we parted ways with Auntie. We informed her the 7 zips were ours. She was able to keep the other zip for herself and do as she pleased with it. We headed back to the North Side to grab the bricks off Gutta-Gutta who was always on standby.

"Yo, what's up lil bros?" Gutta-Gutta said as we entered the crib. His bitch lived in a second-floor apartment by Perry High School.

"Shit trying to get it like you." I said as I shook his hand and took a seat on the couch across from him.

"Shit we're all living in poverty, if I cut my hands off and put yours on its still gone look the same" Gutta-Gutta said as he took a pull on his blunt of purp and swung it our way. I declined it but Don-D toted heavy.

"Ay Keisha bring me four of them thangs." Bad News yelled through the apartment.

"Okay, I got you love." Keisha yelled back to him as she walked in a back room. She brought four blocks wrapped in pages of ripped out porno magazines and placed them on the coffee table.

"Here you go." Keisha said placing them down as Don-D swung her the blunt. She grabbed it and sat on the arm of the couch.

"You got them dollas lil bro?" Gutta-Gutta asked as I dug in my pockets and counting out $800 and handing it to him. He turned around and passed it to Keisha. He sent her to count it one more time. Then she put it up in a safe spot while we bust it up for a few more minutes. We touched on the altercation we had with Gunz and his crew. He found out they referred to themselves as "the Dope Boys", but we already knew that much. This convo reignited the anger for missing Gunz as he ran away. On top of that, Biggie still ain't check when he was hit twice at point blank range.

I took the bricks and placed them in my pocket. We wrapped everything up and headed out the door to go meet Sarah. I called her when we got in the whip and let her know I was in route to her.

I pulled up using the GPS not knowing what to expect. Especially since she told me the front door was unlocked. She expected me to just walk right on into her parent's mansion. I had Don-D sit in the driver seat while I go in here with this work and .45. I didn't know what to expect. It could be a set up to get robbed or some shit with the cops. Everything might be just cool. But I know whatever lies ahead I'm coming back out this front door and getting back in my ride.

"Hello." I said as I turned the doorknob knocking on the door.

"Sales come upstairs." Sarah yelled as she appeared over the top railing. She crept into a room off to the left.

"I'm coming up, where you at?" I asked. I walked up with my gun exposed from my waistline just in case. I moved with caution making my way to the top of the steps. I peeked into the room where the door was cracked. I could hear Sarah from outside.

"Oh my." Sarah screamed jumping back.

"Oh my God, Sales!" Sarah said as she still seemed shaken up.

"Why do you have that thing out?" Sarah asked.

"Oh naw, I don't like surprises. I start to think the worst in unfamiliar situations, my fault." I said as I de-cocked my hammer and put my gun back on my waistline. I covered it up with my shirt as I could tell Sarah was starting to calm down a little bit. She started to relax and the redness in her face was starting to go away.

"I was trying to surprise you with a little quickie if you had time. You know we didn't quite get that far at the hotel." Sarah said as I followed her from the doorway and into her exquisite bedroom. It was grand with a walk-in closet and master bath suite.

"I would be all in baby girl. But I got a shit load of things to take care of this morning. We can definitely take a rain check if you're cool with that." I said. I placed the four bricks, half of zip, and scale on the bed. Then I broke everything down to her number wise.

"Now look, here go your four bricks. You should be selling them for $30 a bag out here so that's 6k for you. If you want to be nice and give deals, you'll break-even at least. That's up to you to figure out along the way. This right here is a half of ounce. I'm gone weigh it for you just to make sure we on the same page. I want 450 back from that then the rest is yours. We'll go from there.

# NAME OF DA GAME

Keep the scale to weigh everything up. Don't try to eyeball nothing because you will cheat yourself out of money. Before I hand you this…" Sarah caught on and went in her top dresser drawer for the $1600. She handed me the money before I could even finish explaining.

"I can take care of your money situation. I guess what's up under my shirt you didn't want. I'll be okay with that rain check just give me a buzz okay." Sarah said with a little melancholy in her voice.

"Oh yeah? Show me what's under that shirt." I asked as I finished counting the money that she handed me.

"Nothing but my kitty kat." Sarah said as she lifted up the bottom of her shirt showing me a nice, shaved pussy. You know like the ones you see in Playboy magazine or something of that sort.

"I'll definitely be calling you later on with the rain check." I said before I gave her another hug and jumped back into the ride and pulled off.

"Everything was cool?" Don-D asked as we drove down the road to exit out of Fox Chapel.

"Yeah, she copped up and was up there trying to give me the pussy. You know there's so much shit that I got to get in order. I don't even have the time to fuck around right now. Come on, let's go to Lexi's spot and count this money." I responded.

## "What to Do?"

## Aug 29, 2005

T he night was so beautiful. It felt like a pre-honeymoon experience. It was time to say goodbye as I dropped D-Weez off downtown. His tour bus met him for the quick drive up the highway to Youngstown, Ohio. He left but he promised to call as much as possible during the next few days until his vacation.

It was time to go home to my pride and joy Malik. I really want to spend some quality time with him." I thought to myself as I cruised home listening to "Make it Last Forever" by Keith Sweat. I was definitely floating on the cloud that D-Weez had put me on. Pulling up to my house seeing Sales' rental made me jump back into the mix of what I was doing.

I quickly reached in my door console for my pre-paid. I picked it up noticing that Gunz hadn't called to at least check up on me. It made me wonder because in my mind I was one kiss away from being his main squeeze. It literally felt like I was one dick suck and a fuck away from knowing where the cash was at. I dropped a quick text to him asking how he was doing and another one saying that I was thinking about him. I wanted him to text or call back when he was free.

I walked through the door greeted by my youngin. He ran to the door jumping into my arms.

"Hey son! Ashanti he wasn't any trouble, was he?" I asked as I picked him up and walked into the living room. I took a seat on the couch next to Ashanti.

"Naw never, that's my lil man. You love Auntie, don't you?" Ashanti said to Malik as he smiled back. He gave her a high five. She smiled but Ashanti's face looked like something was troubling her.

"What's up Ashanti?" I asked as I took notice to the look on my sister's face. I normally don't like her but today is simply different.

"I'm okay sis. What made you ask me that?" Ashanti responded looking to the floor. She didn't believe the words that she spoke herself.

"Bitch really, have you seen your face?" I asked.

"It's just everything that's going on right now. This morning I seen the news about a shooting at the A-Plus/Sunoco. You know the one in Highland Park over by my house. They are searching for Don-D's truck. If it's not his, they want one that looks just like it. This is in connection with the shooting. On top of that Lexi, I'm scared. I'm pregnant and the way things are going I don't want to be raising my child all alone. Shawn just keeps adding fuel to the fire with something that ain't even have to go this far.

"You know what scares me most?" Ashanti asked as her eyes stated to tear up before she continued. "I don't want to end up like you raising a child by myself. I don't want to be forced to stand strong and tall. I'm not trying to be the woman that has to make the best of things. My goal in life is to never give up and be a true success in what I set out to accomplish. To be truthful I really don't want that pressure Lexi. You and mom handled that well but not me." Ashanti said as the tears rolled down her face.

She rushed off to the bathroom before I could even open my mouth to give my input on the situation. I ran in behind her to check on her. She was hunched over and I held her hair as she threw up in the toilet. I rubbed her back with my free hand.

"Are you okay? How far along are you?" I asked.

"Six weeks and I still haven't told Shawn yet. Lexi, I don't know what to do." Ashanti sounded so worried as she explained.

## "Riding Until The End"

## Aug 29, 2005

H e's good but he's going to need lots of rest until his wounds heal. I assume the first shot hit his chest. I'm going to say the second shot is the one that hit his shoulder as he was going down." Dr. Doc said. He was the neighborhood doctor who had performed many malpractices. He used to have his own office until he lost his license for receiving sexual favors from clients. Shortly after that, he was sent off to do a year and a day for selling prescription drugs on the streets. Upon his release, he started working out of his house in the Morningside neighborhood.

"Oh okay, did you hear that nigga? Sit back for a second because everything is cool. Thanks to Dr. Doc." Gunz said to Biggie before thanking the doctor as he walked him to the door. He left Biggie's four-bedroom 2 story brick house and went on his way.

"What the fuck are you talking about nigga? You heard what Dr. Doc said. If it weren't for the fact that I'm fat that nigga would have killed me. B tell him what I'm talking about because he isn't feeling me and what I'm saying right now." Biggie explained and he looked for B-Nasty which is Gunz' little brother to back up what he was saying.

"I feel you Biggie. But you can't do shit. You more of a liability than a factor right now because of your condition. Be happy them slugs hit you on the left because you might not be here." B-Nasty said as he stood up and, walked to the kitchen. He left Biggie, Gunz, and Biggie's second bm DaVita sitting there in the living room quietly. They sat for a minute just reflecting at the words that were just spoken aloud.

"Well like I said I know who the nigga is that owns that white Tahoe. My cousin Nikki be fuckin him and he dropped her off at my mom's crib like a week ago. She said his name was like Don-D or Don-G. I know it was close to that. I heard his right-hand man's name is Sales." DaVita said as she stood up looking at the mirror on the wall. She unwrapped her head scarf revealing her black and red 27-piece.

"I'm waiting on her to hit me back now. As soon as she do, I'll have some more info for y'all to work with." DaVita looked into the kitchen from where she was standing. She could see B-Nasty wiping off .223's Remington bullets with a bandana. He proceeded to load them into a 50-round banana clip of a semi-automatic A-K 47. We call that shit a choppa. He stopped and looked up at her silently then placed his head back down and continued what he was doing.

B-Nasty was an assassin sent straight from hell. His attitude was quiet and real militant. He was the opposite of both Biggie and Gunz because of their flamboyant styles. They also both had a prior run in with the law. The 5'7" light brown skinned low cut 20-year-old had over 10 dead bodies secretly on his jacket. He had mastered what he did best which was to kill. He was willing to kill anybody who crossed his Dope Boy family or served as a threat to his organization. He meant business all day every day.

DaVita's Sprint phone rung a few times before she decided to answer it.

"What you want bitch?" she answered.

"Nothing much bitch, is you still at Biggie's house? I'm on my way over there." Shariece asked.

"You know I'm over here taking care of my Baby Daddy. Where else would I be bitch?" DaVita responded.

"Whatever hoe, I'll be there in like 5 minutes." Shariece stated.

"Bye bitch" DaVita said as she hung up the phone. She sat next to Biggie on the couch rubbing the side of his face. She looked over to Gunz and said to him his bitch is on the way over.

"Who Reese? Ain't nobody thinking about that freak ass bitch." Gunz had just finished his statement before a text came through on his phone from Latoya.

"Hey T.G. I see you've been a lil busy. How did your night finish out last night? I had my first dream about you. You really been on my mind all morning." Gunz read the message for a minute then sat there. He wasn't in the right state of mind to text her back.

Reese walked in the door strutting with her sassiness. She went straight to Biggie showing her sympathy toward his wounds. She dialed back and placed her focus on Gunz who paid her no attention. Him and Latoya texted back and forth. His trap phone started ringing off the hook. Snaps were tweaking for bundles and bricks of dope.

"Okay meet me at the Pittsburgh Zoo in 15 minutes." Gunz kept repeating before hanging up the phone calls and going upstairs. He went into a room where all the bricks were kept inside of a Giant Eagle grocery bag. It was filled with over 100 bricks covered in white rice. This was to keep them dry and to ensure the moisture stays out. Gunz retrieved the 3 orders. One The first one was three bundles, marketing $450 and the second order was for four bundles at $600 The last sell was two bricks. I was letting them go for $1200. He came back downstairs looking for a driver. Reese insisted that she took him to run his errands. No one in the house disagreed. They dipped off and went to go meet everybody in the zoo parking lot.

"So how you been babe?" Sharice asked referring to Gunz as they drove thru traffic.

"I'm not your babe bitch. I'm chillin though." Gunz responded lashing out a lil bit.

"Why you got to keep acting like this towards me? You know those were just some mistakes I made while you were down. I'm confused why can't we work this out? I love and miss you so much." Reese said as they pulled up to a red light. She kept looking for his eyes to lock with hers to show her sincerity to him. But he just kept facing forward and spoke. He wasn't interested in the conversation at all.

"Come on the lights green now." Gunz said before picking up his personal phone and responding to Latoya's question from earlier. We pulled up to a semi full zoo parking lot. He quickly peeped all three cars he was coming to meet parked in various spots in the back of the lot. Gunz cocked his Desert Eagle and tucked it back in his waist as he walked to the different cars to make the transactions.

Shariece sat there as Gunz' phone kept vibrating. She checked and seen the messages from Latoya. She wondered who she was as she picked up the phone and started to read their whole conversation that was texted:

Latoya: Hey T.G. I see you've been a lil busy. How did your night end? I had my first dream about you last night and you've been on my mind all morning.

Gunz: My fault beautiful, some bullshit came up. You had your first dream about me. huh? I guess I'm living up to the hype if that's happening. So how are you?

Latoya: I'm doing good at work, I'm a bit tired from last night with you. I'll be okay. I'm grown and I can handle it. So when am I going to see you again?

Gunz: Well that depends on when you want to see me. I'm a little tied up right now but I'll make an exception for you beautiful.

Latoya: Aww that's so sweet of you to say. So when will you be able to go to another bar with me? I just might have a drink with you this time.

Gunz: I want to say tonight but I'm going to let you catch up on your rest. I'll give the directions to meet me at Hank and Andy's tomorrow night. Does that work for you?

Latoya: Yeah, that's perfect. What time?

Gunz: 9:30, is that too late for you?

Latoya: That's actually perfect.

Gunz: Ok I'll see you later then call me in like an hour or two.

Latoya: Okay will do…

As Shariece read on, her frustration was starting to boil. She placed the phone down on the seat just as Gunz returned to the car.

"Your lil hoe texted you back." said Shariece before pausing for a second.

"So that's who you going to play me out for huh? I ought to smack the shit out of you right now. After all the shit we done been through this is how it is? Who was always in your corner? Who always had your back? Who was it that you trusted with everything? Me, Tommy that's who. Remember what I told you that first night you took me to the gun range after I got my gun license? We went on a date at the overlook of the city. I told you I'm riding to the end. What, that don't mean shit now?" Shariece said as she snapped in the front seat swinging her head back and forth while being all animated.

"No, it don't. Now let's get the fuck out of here I got shit to do." Gunz told her before she put the car in drive as they pulled off.

He started pulling money out of different pockets to count. He stopped for a second and looked over at Reese.

"Look bitch, next time you touch anything of mines I'm going to slap fire out that ass you hear me!" Gunz said before glancing at the tears that ran down her face. He counted his money before they pulled back up to Biggie's house. Gunz got out the car without even saying anything and dropped $50 on her lap. He went into the house as Reese sat in the car crying her heart out.

"He gone play me out for this bitch? She kept repeating this thought over and over inside of her head. Watch I bet I be there tomorrow night. I bet I be there, just watch Tommy. I'll definitely be there." Shariece told herself. She pulled off crying with her heart broken. She was too ashamed to go back into the house.

## "4 Kings & 4 Aces"

## Aug 29, 2005

I played the Young Jeezy "Freestyle" song as Ashanti and I drove back to our house after being away from home for some days. We pulled up and I unloaded our bags. She ran right upstairs and began to undress.

"It feels so good to be back in my own bed." Ashanti said as she flopped down on their therapeutic king size bed.

"I know right, home at last. We ain't staying here long. It's my birthday so get dressed up. We're stepping out in a minute. I already arranged our evening so prep everything you need as well. Get ready now because we're leaving at 8 o'clock." I informed her before I headed to the bathroom picking up my clippers. I had to clean up my cut since I was in between barbershop trips. I came back to the bedroom and Ashanti was laid on the bed with her legs spread like an eagle. All she had on was her panties.

"It's only 5:30 Big Daddy. We ain't got to leave to be wherever until 8. Come get this birthday pussy." Ashanti said as she seductively rubbed her fingers over the top of her clit. She was sticking two fingers inside her pussy then into her mouth. I instantly got rock hard before climbing on top of her kissing and sucking on her lips. I worked my way down to her breasts for a few moments as I gripped her titties in each hand. I slobbered, sucked, and flickered my tongue on her nipples before continuing my journey south as I reached her Georgia Peach.

I kissed and licked her lips slowly before making my way to the top of her clit. I began working my tongue and finding her spot. She was gripping and pulling my ears putting my whole face inside her world. Her body fell back, and she covered her eyes with her hands. I listened as she repeatedly whispered my name softly. She wrapped her legs around my head for a few moments before she tried to stop me.

I was determined to keep pursuit on what I was doing as she lifted her back off the bed. I knew my mission was complete when I felt her legs shaking on my shoulders. She rested her hands on top of my head. Her orgasm passed and I got up and started fuckin her face for a minute. Then I laid her on her back with her legs high in the sky. I fucked the hell out of her like porno sex. I long stroked her like I was Wesley Pipes for a half hour while talking my shit. I bust all over her titties as we finished up.

We went to the bathroom to shower. Ashanti went to the toilet to get most of the nut that would come out. She douched with Summer's Eve and hopped in the shower with me. After showering we got dressed for the night. She took a moment to fix her hair and get final touches added in.

We literally got dressed in just enough time. The limo arrived at 8 o'clock sharp with a bunch of familiar faces already inside. I stepped out in my black tailor-made Perry Ellis suit. It came with a red vest and the red and black tie. And of course, I was stepping in my all-black Stacy Adams. I had on my white gold pinky ring along with my diamond stud white gold bracelet. I also had the matching watch that I ain't never set the time on yet.

Ashanti stepped out ready for the red carpet in a Christian Dior black dress. It hugged her body so perfectly. She had white pearls around her neck and in her ears. She carried a custom made black and white Louis Vuitton pocketbook. Our entourage for the night was Don-D, Trigga Tre, Jamaya, Gutta-Gutta, Keisha, and Lexi. They looked just as fly like they all stepped out of GQ magazine.

We made our way to Station Square on the South Side to board our Gateway Clipper boat trip. It was a little river cruise that was touring up and down the three rivers of my city while they served candlelight dinners. The Gateway Clipper was just a dose of great living. We watched how the city lit up at night as we danced to old school music. They played hits like Earth, Wind & Fire, The O' Jays, and Commodores.

We ate our 5-star meals and smoked weed on the back balcony. The drinks were flowing and we mingled with each other all night long. We were living like there was no tomorrow. It was like escaping the drama for some hours which eased my mind. I looked at all of us genuinely enjoying ourselves. For a moment we were able to forget about everything else that was going on. I was ready to make my toast as we stood on the upper deck just cooling with the breeze.

"Aye can I have y'all attention please?" I asked while raising my voice and tapping on my champagne glass to get my whole squad's attention. A few onlookers that were close to us on the back balcony listened up too as I spoke my words.

"Damn look at all y'all. Shit look at all of us. I want to thank y'all for coming out tonight and celebrating me and Don-D's birthday/ We appreciate yall coming to fuck with us. Much love to y'all and I know we got shit going on in our lives but tonight was well needed for me. It was a good night to celebrate with y'all. Tre, Gutta, D, I'd give my life for y'all with pride. Ashanti, Maya, Keisha, and Lex, y'all have my utmost respect and gratitude. Y'all loyalty to us shows a lot. Instead of referring to y'all as Queens I'm going give y'all the title of Aces. Y'all four the reason behind of all of the success of a king. I'm toasting to that. Here we are, 4 Kings & 4 Aces. I love y'all." I preached before we toasted and enjoyed the rest of our evening on the boat.

## "The Phone Conversation"

## Aug 29, 2005

W hat's up cuz? What you been up to?" DaVita happily asked Nikki and waited for a response.

"Nothing cuz, I'm just chilling. How's your mom, sisters, and my adorable lil cousin doing?" Nikki asked as she engaged in conversation with her big cousin.

"Good, everybody has been asking about you. We haven't seen or heard from you in a week. Matter fact the last time I seen you was when you got dropped off over my mom's house. What's dude name that brought you over here?" DaVita spoke while acting dumb like she forgot dude's name.

"Who are you talking about? Don-D?" Nikki asked.

"Yeah, that's his name the one with the truck, right?" DaVita shot back. She was baiting her cousin on her game she was running. Nikki wasn't hip to anything that was going on. She was just freely giving up the information.

"Yeah, that's him." Nikki responded.

"Okay girl, I see you boo loving. So how did you meet him?" DaVita asked.

"Naw it ain't all that serious between us. He so caught up in the streets and his football career. You know how these niggas out here are scared of a commitment. I think I'm starting to wear him down. His mom lives two doors up the street from my mom. Every night he's home he makes sure he calls me to get some of this "Nikilicous". He'll even come get me from my dad's or wherever I am girl. He says just to has to have me next to him when he wakes up in the morning." Nikki bragged.

"Shit I hear that girl." DaVita laughed with her as she was just informed on all she needed to tell her baby daddy. They kept the conversation going on for a few minutes. DaVita said she would hook up with her later to go eat and ended the call. After hanging up she went straight to tell her baby daddy and his boys all the info she had just gotten from her cousin Nikki. B-Nasty then gave her some money to take her cousin Nikki out on a date. He threw her the keys to his black Crown Vic sitting on 24's and suicide scissor doors.

*"I got a plan."*

## Aug 29, 2005

D amn girl you fucked up." Trigga Tre' said as he watched his baby momma Jamaya stumble to make it to the railing. The rest of us on looked from limo laughing as we pulled up to the Double Tree hotel.

"Tre, help your girl before she hurts herself." Ashanti said as she wrapped her hand around my waist for leverage as we walked toward the front entrance of the hotel.

We got up to our suites and settled our ladies in first. I had all the men come to my suite while Ashanti was in the shower. I'm sure that's what the other women were doing too. You know the first thing they do is hop right in the shower when they come in from outside.

"Yo, what's up lil bro? You gotta to make this quick. I'm about to do a lot of fuckin before these beans leave my system tonight." Bad News said as he led the others into my suite and shutting the door behind them.

"My fault y'all but this shit been on my mind all day. I got a plan. I want to make sure we all in together with the same motives." I said.

"Yeah? What are you talking about?" Trigga Tre said as he started rubbing his hands together.

"The beef with these dickheads started one way. When it first occurred, it was personal. Now it's business." I said as everybody looked dumb founded then I began to break it down.

"See the Dope Boys collectively get money and do whatever else they do. What I'm thinking now is that we kill them all and everybody affiliated with them. We can shut the whole area down and after a month or two the smoke will clear. We'll be able to sew that whole area up and then some. So, what's the deal? Y'all with it?" I asked.

"Hell mothafuckin yea nigga! What these tattoo's say on the inside of my arms nigga? 'Bout Money' so let's get money my nigga" Gutta-Gutta said as we all splowed each other up before all heading back to their suites.

Since we all agreed on the same plan it was only a matter of time before we would put it in place and act upon it. Right now, it was time to turn all phones off because it was time to do what we all came to do. We split back up with our ladies. All I could think was it's about to be a movie up in my shit. We gone fuck each other's brains out. Hopefully, Don-D was finally going to be able to hit Lexi.

## "The Gloves Are Off"

## Aug 30, 2005

S hawn wake up!!" Ashanti said as she kept shaking my arm messing up the dream I was having. I was on Daytona Beach enjoying spring break all over again just me, my dick, and balls. I was surrounded by all the beautiful women. All the Brazilians, Mexicans and Puerto Ricans a nigga could ever wish for.

"Shawn wake up, wake up before I bite it off!" Ashanti said as she grabbed my dick from under the sheets.

"Oh, damn bae." I said as I rolled over and out of the bed.

"Shawn quit playing all the time come on and take a shower with me so we can go to the diner and get some breakfast." Ashanti whined like a lil baby as she sprawled out across the bed looking so seductive. Her hair was all over the place from the wild sex we had the night before. I looked down at my dick where the dried up cum had left stains.

"Yeah, I busted your ass last night." I said bringing a lil humor and cockiness to the situation.

"I couldn't tell for real cause less than 5 minutes after me riding you from the back, your black ass was sleep. Who put it on who Boo-Boo?" Ashanti said shooting back the same humor and cockiness I just spat to her. She hopped out of the bed steady grinning and shit. She strutted her stuff all the way toward the bathroom.

"Oh and Sales, you was moaning in your sleep and calling my name. I definitely put it on you. I'll be in the shower waiting for you to come wash my back sweetheart." Ashanti said as she disappeared into the bathroom while I sat there thinking. I waited a few minutes before joining her. I know how she likes to have the first couple minutes of bathroom time to herself. She has to do her "womanly things" as she calls it.

After showering we got dressed or fresh as I like to call it. We all met down in the lobby with our bags. We hopped in the limo and headed to breakfast. She had decided on DeLuca's diner in the Strip District.

We sat and waited on our food. Don-D stayed locked into his phone while the rest of us conversed.

"Yo bro, you ok?" I asked him.

"Naw I've been trying to get in touch with mom all morning and she ain't call or text back yet." Don-D said in a discomforted voice.

"You already know how she is bro. Everything is on her time. Why is you tripping bro?" I asked.

"Naw because last night I had a nightmare with my mom in it. I ain't dreamt no shit like that before. I just ain't been able to write it off as a bad dream as much as I been trying to all morning." Don-D stated.

"Iight bet well let's just take a detour over there before we all get dropped off. That'll put an end to all the speculation in your mind. Is that cool bro?" I asked as Don-D nodded his head agreeing with me. Then he started engaging in conversation with everyone until the food arrived.

"We gone take this detour. Ain't nobody in a rush, are y'all?" I asked. They all responded go head, do you. We cruised over to Momma Mace's house keeping the party going. We all decided we were going to go in once seeing her cream Lincoln Navigator parked out front.

"Oh, she probably in the shower with the music on if she can't hear. Nevaeh stayed over her friend's house from school. I grabbed the key from my suitcase. Hold up." Don-D said as we stood there as my knocking went unattended to.

"Mom, where you at?" Don-D yelled through the house as we all walked in.

"What the fuck happened in here?" I said as I looked around the living room noticing it was dismantled and things thrown around. Don-D took one look at me before taking off up the steps not saying anything. I ran up behind him looking for Momma Mace as we ended up in front of Momma Mace's bedroom door. The door was cracked as Don-D busted in only to see Momma Mace lying in the floor in a pool of blood with a .357 right next to her body. It was a towel covering half of her bottom which indicated she may have been drying off.

"Fuck man" Don-D said as he punched a hole into the drywall. I just stood there in disbelief. Everyone came running up the steps and seeing Momma Mace laying there dead.

"Oh my God Shawn!" Ashanti said as she came close to me putting her head into my chest.

"What the fuck, my fucking Auntie cuz. Oh niggas is gone fuckin pay, niggas is fuckin dead." Trigga Tre' said as he stood there shaking his head agreeing with himself. A blank look came back to his face.

"I'm about to call 911." Ashanti said as she started to walk away.

"Hold up a second, give us like 5 minutes. Once them boys get here they gone tear this place apart. They are ransacking and any and everything." Bad News said as he walked over picking up the dirty harry that had something covering the front part of the barrel.

"What the fuck is on it?" I asked

"Whoever did this is not an amateur. This pistol has the serial numbers scratched off and the handle is duck taped. They even put a silencer on a .357." Gutta-Gutta announced.

"How the fuck do you silence a .357 and take 5 shots? You don't even get 5 shots with the watermelon on a pump." I asked stating the only thing that I ever saw somebody do. I didn't really know the ins and outs of the riding shit.

"See this shit right here is part of the cushion you sit on in your car seats. This shit right here can silence any of the craziest hammers. That's why nobody could hear this big ass gun going off." Bad News taught us like he was a professor at Harvard or some shit.

"Man fuck that shit, come on. Let's get everything so we can get this shit out of here. We need to start planning how everything going down." Trigga Tre' snapped before we started going through the house and taking bags of money and a few guns to the limo.

"Aight baby girl, go head and call the cops now." I said as I took one more good look at Momma Mace and the enormous bullet holes in her body. Bad News then wrapped da .357 up in a towel then placed it in a book bag. He walked out to the limo silently.

"Aye babe you stay here with Don-D. The rest of us are going to take off. I'll be here to pick you'll up later." I said before pausing then looking at Don-D. I was trying to find the right words to say to him about his mother. Shit she was our mother to be honest. Nothing came out, I just gave a look that I was hoping conveyed we gone burn hell down about this. I turned around and took off down the steps before Don-D called out my name.

NAME OF DA GAME

"What's up bro?" I responded turning around.

"Da gloves are off now." Don-D said I seen the fire burning of death in his eyes. I just nodded back then walked to the limo and got inside. We had the limo driver drop everybody off at their homes. Me and Lexi got dropped off at her spot. Bad News and Trigga Tre said they would meet up with us in a couple of hours. I started to think who could have got to her and how? I thought back and remembered we were in Don-D's truck. How they found out where the spot was is what I wondered." I said to myself trying to come up with answers.

"What's up Boo?" Lexi said as we walked into the crib. She was on the phone with that nigga Gunz playing shit smooth.

"What's up baby girl?" he responded.

"Nothing, I'm getting ready for a meeting before I call my travel agent." Lexi shot at him playing as if she was Latoya.

"Your travel agent for what?" Gunz asked.

"I want to take you on a trip with me if you don't mind?" Lexi asked. I stood there all into her conversation as she looked into my eyes.

"You for real, where you want to go?" Gunz responded knowing all that was happening on his end. He thought about how he only ever left the city three times. Two were business trips to his plug and the other one was juvenile placement.

"I want to go away for two weeks after my meeting in New York. I'm overdue for a vacation to the Bahamas. Can you come with me please? The whole trip is on me baby." Lexi asked buttering him up.

"Yea we can do that but..." Gunz started to speak before she cut him off.

"But nothing baby and don't worry about your situation. I'm already putting the woodworks together for your alias, okay?" Lexi said.

"Cool, well I see you get what you want. You're real aggressive and I like that." Gunz said. You could tell the way the words slid off his lips he was feeling himself now.

"I got to baby. Ain't too many men of your caliber out here left that are genuine. I have to lock you down before I let somebody take what's mines or what could be." Lexi said as she put a sweet lil innocent voice on.

"Okay I agree with you there. Well Latoya, I'm going to let you go. I got some errands to run. I'll give you a call later to give you directions. Is that cool with you?" Gunz asked.

"Yea that's fine with me boo. I'll talk to you later." Lexi said before hanging up the phone. She climbed up on the couch behind me and started massaging my head. She worked her way to my neck and back. It felt so fucking good.

"He wants to meet at some bar called Hank and Andy's off of Negley Ave around 9:30. I figured I'd go. I'll let you know who's there once I scope out the scene. Once I see whose all in the building, I'll text you. Does that work for you?" Lexi asked.

"Yeah, that'll work. Just be my eyes on the inside and I got it from there." I said as I sparked the half of blunt that sat in the ashtray. Lexi continued to massage my back while I thought about Momma Mace.

## "Getting the Punk Ass Cops Involved"

## Aug 30, 2005

S ir the body is upstairs." a blue suit officer said as Detective E. Banks walked through the house. They had been on the partners for 6 years. They went ahead straight upstairs where Macy Dixon lied. Everyone in the room played a different role. Whether they were taking pictures, examining, or fingerprinting. It turned into a whole investigation instantaneously.

What do you think?" Det. Grove asked his partner Det. E. Banks as she squatted over the dead body.

"We know 5 shots rules out it being an accident. Second thing is the house really wasn't too displaced for a robbery. Especially with the diamonds left on the dresser. I'd say, this killing was personal." Det. E. Banks said as she stood up looking at her partner.

"Look closely at the size of these bullet wounds. I'm going to say these were shots fired from a .357 magnum point blank range. My better judgment tells me this shot in the shoulder was first. It seems like it came from the distance of the doorway. Check how far the blood is over on the wall. The second shot must have dropped her. I say that because these 3 shots over here look perfectly aligned. Almost as if she were being stood over top of." Detective Grove pointed out as he picked up a piece of the cushion with tweezers and dropped into an evidence bag.

"And what I don't understand is how 5 shots could go off and nobody report anything. How could this woman just be sitting here for a least 10 hours?" Detective E. Banks said as they walked back down the steps. They headed right over to a group of regular uniform officers.

"We have a few questions. What's her name? Who reported and found her body? Has anybody started questioning neighbors yet?" Det. E. Banks asked.

"Her name was Macy Dixon she was only 32 with two kids. Her body was found by her 16-year-old son and his friend earlier this morning. They are both over there sitting in the back of a cruiser. Their names are Donald Dixon and Ashanti Jackson. He is 16 and she is 24. The neighbors haven't been any help yet as they all say they haven't seen nothing. They say she was well liked, no drama, no boyfriend that they have seen. They say they didn't see anything strange over here last night. And not one person heard any shots." recited the officer as he read what he had in his memo pad.

"She's a little too old to be hanging with a 16-year-old. Okay thank you and have some officers question these neighbors again. Somebody must have seen or heard something. They keep looking out their windows and some of them have even formed an onlooking crowd on the opposite side of the street." Det. E Banks stated as her and Det. Grove walked over to the police cruiser to speak to Don-D and Ashanti.

"Mr. Dixon, Ms. Jackson, I'm homicide detective Grove and this is my partner Detective Banks. Do you mind if we have a word with you two down at the station? I know this is a devastating time for you. We just need to find out all we can to bring your mother's tragedy to justice." Detective Grove asked.

"Yeah, we'll go." Don-D said before Detective Grove shut the cruiser door. He ordered a patrol officer to take them down to homicide. She stayed behind and gathered some more information before going down to question them.

Don-D and Ashanti were separated and placed in different rooms once they arrived at the station. Ashanti was asked little questions, but it really was not any use because Ashanti already knew the rules of the game. It really wasn't much of a story to make up. Then came the interview with Don-D. He was definitely agitated at the whole process.

"Is this going to take all day?" he asked. He looked at the double mirror that sat to the left of his seat. He stared knowing there were cops on the other side of the glass watching him like a suspect of his own mother's murder. And he was crying tears hoping to get a moment alone.

"Sorry it took so long. Things get crazy around here come summertime." said Det. Grove as he entered the room. He was 6'4 and weighed like 330 lbs. He took a seat on the other side of the table. The interrogation lasted for three and a half hours as they came in one at a time. The detectives came in together playing the good cop, bad cop role. They asked about his father Big Sherm and what was his mother into. They kept trying to ask questions in as many ways as possible. They started insinuating that this was a retaliation on account of something Trigga Tre' had done in the past.

The interviews were broken up by his Uncle Kevin when he arrived at the homicide headquarters. They were immediately released because of illegal questioning. They let him take them home with no issue since he was next of kin to Momma Mace. He was her older brother. All he did was go to work and come home to his family. He had a wife named Mya and they had twin girls that were six months old. He was never in the streets. He was clueless on how to approach the situation about his sister's murder.

"Donald, are you okay?" Uncle Kevin asked as they stepped outside of the homicide headquarters. Ashanti was already outside waiting for them.

"Naw Unc, they took my mom." Don-D said as he walked over to Ashanti embracing her with a hug before facing his uncle again.

"I need your phone right quick Unc. We gave our phones to Sales because these crackers be on some funny shit. You know they good for searching and tapping phones." Don-D explained as they all walked to his uncle Kevin's Chevy Malibu. They pulled off from the scene.

"Sales, what's up?" Don-D said talking on the phone.

"Shit waiting on Trigga and Gutta to get here then I'm putting this shit together. Where y'all at and whose phone is this?" I asked.

"This is Uncle Kev's phone. He just picked us up. We're on our way to go pick up my baby sister before we part ways." Don-D responded.

"Aight bet. But I want y'all to just chill at Uncle Kev's crib until tomorrow morning. I'll break it down to you in the a.m." I suggested.

"Naw fuck that." Don-D started to snap before being cut off by me.

"Naw, I got this just chill out." I said.

"Chill out?" Don-D responded as if I just insulted him or something before he went in on me.

"They just took my fuckin mom. You expect me to fuckin chill? What I look like a bitch to you nigga?"

"What the fuck you mean nigga I feel the same fuckin way. This is chess not checkers. Use your fuckin head cuz." I snapped back.

"I ain't trying to hear that shit. I'm ready to die about this nigga. Fuck what you talking about cuz." Don-D said with so much anger in his words. I could feel they were straight from his heart.

"Well one was more than enough in my books so fall the fuck back." I responded.

"Man fuck you." Don-D yelled before hanging up the phone. His temperature kept rising until he was damn near foaming at the mouth. He sat in the back while Ashanti kept looking back at him from the front seat. She just watched not knowing what to say to try and make him feel better. She decided to just keep quiet in that moment.

## "Let's Finish the Job"

## Aug 30, 2005

Aye yall I'm cooling off tonight. I'm going to go chill with Latoya for a minute." Gunz informed B-Nasty and Biggie.

"Bro I don't think that's a clever idea. We just struck first in a war." B-Nasty said as Biggie kept nodding his head agreeing with what B-Nasty was saying.

"Naw it's cool, they shit hot man. They can't move like they really want to since those eyes are on them. We up one right now for sure. On top of that we only going to that spot off of Negley Ave for a couple of drinks. Then we gone slide back over this way for a while." Gunz informed.

"Bro I really don't think that's too smart. I mean I ain't trying to soulja hate on you but let's finish the job." B-Nasty replied.

"You right and I feel you. When you let beef sit that's when shit goes bad. I just need a couple of hours to go chill. I'll be back soon." Gunz shot back.

"Ok Casanova go head. But make sure y'all slide over here because we still ain't never met this bitch." B-Nasty said as he pounded his brother up before Gunz walked out the door. He was heading home to hop in the shower and get dressed up before he left to meet Latoya.

## "Time to Boot"

## Aug 30, 2005

A ye where is Malik at?" I asked as I know I haven't seen him or heard her say two words about him since I've been over here.

"He's over at his Auntie's house. Lexi responded referring to Nha'Lisa. That was Coc's older sister who takes him every chance she gets.

"Oh aight, well get up and get ready." I said as I laid on my stomach as she kept giving me a massage all over my body as I laid there in my boxers.

"Okay well you get up too before your boys get here or my sister pop back up." Lexi said as she got off my back giving me a chance to stand up. I instantly felt the difference in how tense I was. Trigga Tre and Bad News showed up at the crib about ten minutes later.

"What's up cuz?" I said as I embraced both with handshakes letting them into the house.

NAME OF DA GAME

"Shit chilling, did little cuz make it back yet? I know them crackers probably brought them in for questioning and shit." Trigga Tre asked.

"Yeah, he did but I advised him and Ashanti to fall back over your dad's house. Him and his wife's spot was the most low key right now." I told Trigga Tre.

"Oh ok, yea that's cool because everything is under control around here." Trigga Tre' responded.

"Y'all bring them choppas and the ride?" I asked.

"Yeah, I had my youngin steal this minivan with the glow ring and change this license plate so we're good. I grabbed 2 AK's with beams plus I brought out my AR with the blue beam. It has the shell catcher on it. Nevertheless, these are Teflon vests and we can't afford no fuck ups." Bad News said.

"We got the gas in there too along with some sweatpants and bleach." Trigga Tre added.

"Aight bet, we gone chill here until Lexi leave then we gone stake out somewhere close by. This pussy dead and so is anybody else affiliated with him." I said as they sat on the couch twisting blunts. We heard Lexi down the hall running the blow dryer prepping herself. About an hour later Lexi was on her way out the door to go meet Gunz. We were all dressed up in our throw away black dickie jumpsuits. We jumped in the minivan and took off.

☐

## "Bar Meeting"

## Aug 30, 2005

H ey how you handsome? You look so good right now."
Lexi said as she checked out Gunz. He was sporting a
black wife beater, some Red Monkey jeans, and a pair of
black ACGs. He rocked a 2inch diamond studded
bracelet with the 2.0 CT diamond pinky ring.

"You look so beautiful tonight. I'm stunned in a daze right
now staring at you." Gunz complimented as he took a step back to
admire Lexi. She had on a black skirt, a beige Burberry button up,
6-inch stiletto pumps and the matching Burberry bag. She had a
gold inch and half herringbone around her neck.

"Oh stop it, so how you been?" Lexi asked seeming
flattered by his compliments.

"I've been stressed out with so much shit going on lately.
So how you been?" Gunz replied and asked.

"Just work and more work. Working hard until we can go on this vacation. I guess we both can use it now huh?" Lexi said before they both let out a giggle together.

"Yeah, that sounds like a plan. So what made you want to bring me on a vacation with you?" Gunz replied.

"Well first off I've been working hard trying to build my career. I've been finding you real intriguing lately. I just want to kick back and get to know you one on one. You know, without distractions and interruptions. So, what you think?" Lexi asked.

"Yea we can do that." said Gunz as they small talked for a few minutes. Lexi sipped her Coors Light and Gunz took two Long Island Iced Teas down. Lexi felt he was getting comfortable enough to start asking questions.

"So this is your hang out spot huh? Where your boys and everybody else? Ain't too many people here tonight." Lexi asked as she looked around the bar.

"Naw I really don't fuck with a lot of people that slide in here except Mia. She's the bartender right over there. My niggas usually come here with me but not tonight. I wanted to just fall back with the two of us." Gunz said trying to be in touch with his sensitive side.

"Oh, that was so sweet." Lexi said reaching across the table and kissing Gunz on his lips. She excused herself from the table to go use the bathroom.

Once in the bathroom Lexi pulled her main phone out of her purse and sent a text to Sales.

"It's only us here. We're leaving in 20 minutes. Make sure you're ready and on point time-wise baby." She said. Lexi returned to her seating area only to find Gunz gone.

"He'll be right back. He just stepped outside to his car right quick." the bartender Mia yelled across the bar. Lexi nodded back to acknowledge she heard her. She went to the bar ordering two double shots of Hennessy and two Long Islands. She sat the drinks on the table. With her back to the crowd, she reached inside her handbag and pulled out a mickey. She dropped it into one of the double shots. Her back was turned away from the rest of the bar crowd. She swirled it with the skinny straw to get it all mixed in. Moments later Gunz came walking back into the bar and sat back in his seat.

"My fault babe. I had to handle something right quick. What's all this about?" Gunz asked as he looked at the drinks on the table.

"Come on baby, we gone take a shot and sip our Coronas. We can talk here for a little longer then it's gone be time for us to roll. Lexi informed as she slid the mickey drink in front of Gunz. They toasted to the two of them before taking the shots back.

"Oh my gosh, Tommy I'm going to be hung over in the morning. Are you going to take care of me?" Lexi asked Gunz.

"What?" Gunz asked as he started to rub his face.

"Come on, let's go I'ma need my booty rubbed and trash bag." Lexi said as she pretended to be a lil drunk too. She walked over to Gunz to start helping him up. She noticed the bullet proof vest he had on. She also seen the gun on his waist as they headed to the front door.

"Y'all sure y'all gone be okay? Y'all are both hit." Mia asked. She was referring to how drunk Gunz looked.

"We're going to be fine. Thanks for asking." Lexi replied looking down. She never lifted her head up until she passed the front counter where the bartender was.

"No problem that's my boy. I'm just making sure y'all okay. By the way, my name is Mia." the bartender said.

"My name is Latoya nice to meet you." Lexi said as she walked out the front door as Gunz mumbled something.

"What you say babe?" Lexi asked.

NAME OF DA GAME

"What the fuck is wrong with me? I'm fucked up." Gunz stated as they started to approach his ride. She looked up and noticed two figures in all black walking toward them. All you could see in the dark shadows of the night were big objects in their hands. I noticed the demeanor coming towards me and realized it was Sales and Gutta-Gutta approaching. Gunz' head remained down the whole time they walked toward his ride.

"Hold on baby I'll be right back I got to run to my truck real quick." Lexi said as she took off heading toward her truck.

Gunz was still dumbfounded and lost. That mickey had him fucked up. He looked up just as the first shot was fired with a .223. His body went spinning sideways then multiple gun shots rang out and he collapsed. Then the two stood over top of Gunz' body letting off 20 more up close. So closed it was knocking pieces of his body off during impact. They both took off back into the dark.

## "It Was a Fucking Set Up"

## Aug 30, 2005

I can't believe this nigga trying to play me out. If this bitch in here I'm going to fuck her up." Shariece said to herself as she pulled up in front of Hank and Andy's. She hopped out her car with Vaseline on her face, earrings out of her ears, and her hair tied up. She had a Swiss blade and mace in her hands. Of course she had on gloves too. She had on some sweatpants and Air Max 95s. Her whole get up sent one message. She was ready and willing to fight for what she felt was hers.

"What's up Gunz? Where your bitch at?" Shariece asked as she walked up on him. He sat there with a disgusted look on his face. He couldn't stand her ass.

"What the fuck is you doing here Shariece?" Gunz asked.

"No where's your lil bitch at? I know she here because there's a Coors Light beer bottle right across from your seat. I know she here. Where she at? In the bathroom?" Shariece said as she started to walk toward the ladies' room. Gunz stopped her in her tracks and grabbed her by the arm.

"Shariece get the fuck out of here before I lose my cool." Gunz snapped.

"Before you lose your cool…" Shariece mimicked him.

"What you gone do Gunz? You gone shoot me? Nigga I'll fuck your ass up in here." Shariece said raising her voice as she attempted to swing at him. Gunz jumped out of his seat and gripped her up. He escorted her out of the bar and back to her car.

"I can't fuckin believe you're trying to play me after all this." Shariece said as Gunz continued to pull her by her arm to her car.

"Get the fuck out of here. You know how I feel about you. You're nothing but a nasty smut bucket bitch." Gunz said to her through his teeth as Shariece stood there trying to hold back her tears. He turned and walked away and never looked back.

Shariece got in her car still sitting there trying to think of her next move. She kept replaying in her head that she really fucked up with the love of her life. It was to the point Gunz wasn't ever going to forgive her.

Shariece just sat there crying as she spotted Gunz and his mystery bitch Latoya walking out of the bar. As they were heading toward his car, she caught a glimpse of two men in all black. She seen the shadow from the headlights of a passing car. Latoya walked off leaving Gunz standing there by himself. He was looking drunk and staggering. The gun shots rang out as Shariece screamed out Gunz name. She was screaming but couldn't move because her body froze in fear. The choppas went off for what seemed like forever.

Once the firing had stopped, she watched the men disappear back into the night. She looked over and noticed Latoya's truck was already gone. Shariece ran over to Gunz body. It was hard to even recognize him. Half of his head was missing while the rest of his body looked like a noodle strainer.

"Oh my God! Tommy why? Tommy why?" Shariece said as she held what was left Gunz in her arms. He laid there looking back up at her. People started to crowd around while she sat in a puddle of blood and slugs.

"Call a fuckin ambulance somebody!" yelled Shariece. The tears flowed down her face as the thought to herself it was a fuckin set up. She snapped out and went into shock.

## "Got to Pay the Cost to Be the Boss"

## Aug 31,2005

H ello." I said picking up the phone realizing it was 5:40 in the morning.

"Neph where you at?" said Pimp.

"I'm on the North Side. Why? What's up Unc?" I responded.

"Aight, Unc city bound so stop past spot A. Then meet me over at spot P A.S.A.P." Pimp said.

"Aight bet I'm on it." I responded knowing it had to be especially important for it to be this early in the morning. It seemed urgent and whatever it was it made him come back from out of town early.

I cruised through the streets vibing early morning. I went by Spot A and his sister was wide awoke smoking cigarettes. I popped out and went directly to spot P. That was Pimp's whore house. I couldn't figure out what was going on. Nothing was clear and I knew something wasn't right.

I pulled up and two of Pimp's whores met me outside to walk me in. Pimp sat at his dining room table. The look on his face automatically told me that something was wrong.

"What's up Unc?" I asked.

"Sit down Neph." Pimp said as he sipped on his glass of moonshine then spoke on.

"Now you know I been hearing about what's been going on round here lately. First off, I want to say I'm sorry to hear about Macy. I just hope you learned a lesson in the Art of War. Is everything finished now?"

"Naw I didn't finish yet but…" I started to say before Pimp cut me off.

"There ain't no but. You give your enemy no air to breathe. If you smother a fire it's going to go out. If you give it air to reignite then shit like this is going to happen. It'll become bigger and harder to contain. Think of how out west there are those big ass forest fires that just keep spreading. The way the fire department contains them is they take the air away. They accomplish this by starting and putting out small fires all around the big fire. This kills its way to spread and the fire dies because it runs out of oxygen. Take a moment and think about that.

Now I could easily dead the situation for you by sending my troops to show you how it's done. But I'm not going to always be around to fight your battles for you. I'm aiming to make you my successor when I'm done with the game if you can handle it. And I know who you can be which is a boss. You going to go through shit like this in the future because there's nothing but wolves, snakes, and potential lions in this jungle. The thing is they have limits. You a boss ain't no such thing as limits. So, go handle your business and get at me when you done aight?" Pimp said to me.

"Aight bet say no more" I responded as I shook his hand. Nothing more needed to be said. I headed for the front door right before Pimp called my name one last time.

NAME OF DA GAME

"What's up Pimp?" I responded.

"You gotta pay the cost to be the boss." He said.

□

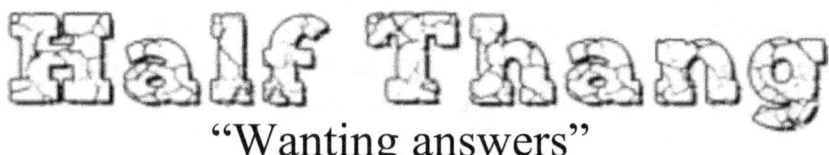

## "Wanting answers"

# Aug 31, 2005

T his is Channel 11 breaking news. This incident occurred last night out front of a bar in Highland Park around 10:30pm. 40 shell casings were recovered on the scene of the shooting. Police are not yet releasing the victim's name until his family members are notified. It was reported that two men with assault rifles shot him 30 plus times. The gentleman was pronounced dead on the scene. If you'd like to make a report involving this crime, please call the number at the bottom of the screen. The police need any and all assistance." said the new reporter before going on about some other shootings around the city.

"Shariece what the fuck happened?" B-Nasty asked.

"I already told you B. I went down there to the bar. When I walked in, he was sitting alone. We started arguing off the rip. He threatened me and kicked me out. I got in my car crying then a few minutes later they came out. He was leaning on that bitch in front of his car for a minute. Then I looked up and she had left him standing there. That's when the two dudes ran up. They shot him and ran off. When I got to him, I looked around and that bitch was gone too." Shariece cried out. B-Nasty slapped her to the ground and screamed "Bitch you better not be lying to me."

"B, I'm not. I swear to God. You know I'm in love with your brother. He was my heart and soul. You know I wouldn't do that. B, please don't hurt me." Shariece said as the tears rolled down her face. She instantly became frightened for her life. She didn't really know what to expect next from B-Nasty. Sometimes he would just snap out because he didn't have it all. With his brother being murdered he was going to make everybody pay with their lives. It was written all over his face.

"Aye Big, call Skeedi and Chewy for me. Tell them I said I'll be over to pick them up in a half hour." B-Nasty said as he went upstairs to change his clothes. He grabbed two Uzi's out of the drop tile ceiling from out of his room and cleaned the barrels on them. He headed out the door with Biggie who was wobbling to the car with the 12 gauge inside of an unzipped duffle bag.

He pulled up in front of lil Skeedi and Chewy's apartment building and the two came right out. They hopped in the back with Big and B-Nasty.

"What's up Nast and Big?" the boys said as the two 15-year-olds shook hands.

"What's good man? Aye was y'all by the bar last night grinding?" B-Nasty asked.

"Naw we were over here waiting on your brother to drop off these bricks. Shit we've been missing money all night and morning because he still ain't came through yet. But I did get a call from my mom saying some shit about somebody shooting down there last night." responded Chewy.

"Some bitch ass niggas ran down on my brother. Aye I want y'all to keep y'all eyes and ears open to the streets. Report everything y'all hear about this back to me aight lil homies?" B-Nasty asked as he passed them back the blunt of Haze that he was smoking on. Biggie passed them back a stack and 10 bricks telling them that was for them. They took the money, work and the blunt and hopped out the ride.

B-Nasty talked to his mom and got word that a few detectives stopped past her crib. They came asking questions and wouldn't give up Gunz cell phone. They say they were using it for evidence towards the case they were working on. They claim they were hoping a lead would come about. They wanted to talk to B-Nasty hoping he could provide some type of info to help them crack this case.

B-Nasty and Biggie then started to drive around hoping to get lucky to find these niggas or any niggas they didn't fuck with. JD and B-Nasty already didn't give a fuck as he drove past Don-D's mom's house like six times. Then the idea popped in his head to go holla at Mia that bartended that night. The thought of the words Shariece said played over and over in his head. The fact that Gunz' date Latoya left him standing there. Once the gunfire ended, she was gone and it was Shariece there with him. Either she set him up with the backdoor or she was scared for her life. It could of went either way honestly.

"Only if I had gone with my gut feeling that I should have met the bitch first. I should of still went and checked on him at the bar. Shit would've ended differently. And if not, I'd at least have a face to track down for answers instead of being at square one." B-Nasty thought to himself. The song that he was listening to by Soulja Slim and B.G. put more evil thoughts in his head. Their ride continued in silence until they reached Mia's house.

## "Oh Shit, Ima Be a Daddy"

## August 31, 2005

W ho dis?" I asked as a number popped up that I didn't recognize.

"Shawn it's me. I'm still at Don-D's Uncle's house. Like a half hour ago detectives came by here. They took him and his uncle down to the police station for questions." Ashanti informed me.

"Aight babe this is what I want you to do. Get dressed and meet me at the crib but catch a cab." I instructed Ashanti.

I remembered a text I received from Auntie Michelle saying she was running low. I replied back that I'll be there soon. I planned to slide over there until Ashanti informed me about Don-D going down for questioning again. I had to give Ashanti a pep talk and make sure alibies were in place. Just in case worse comes to worst, we needed to be safe. And now is not the time for flaws or anything unnecessary to unfold. Anything leaving me bewildered with chances higher to go to jail or death is for the birds.

I was leaving Bad News' crib where we all got high and fucked these lil stripper bitches to take our minds off what happened earlier. My adrenaline was pumping so hard before the shooting. There was no way I wasn't going to kill him that night. Even afterwards it didn't heal the pain I felt in my heart for Momma Mace. Knowing she wasn't going to be around anymore, wasn't justice enough.

It's about a twenty-minute drive to get from the North Side back to my house. I just seen the empty cab riding past me giving me confirmation that Ashanti made it home safe.

"Aye Babe where you at?" I asked as I walked through the front door. She came from behind our bedroom door. I could see all the stress in her face and how tired she was.

"Shawn what are we going to do about Don-D going back down for questioning? What if they on to y'all? I swear I can't lose you right now and these murders are happening. What if they try to give you a life sentence? What if you get killed behind all this bullshit? Shawn I am starting to lose my mind. I'm pregnant and I don't want to lose this baby behind worrying about your black ass." Ashanti blurted out as she looked inside my eyes.

I was left speechless, in shock and happy as hell. But at the moment I was too worried for her and my seed to really show it. I just grabbed her and hugged her tight. I assured her everything was going to be okay. I let her know that we were going to make it. She took a step back from me to look into my eyes again and seen my sincerity. Tears started running down her face.

"Come here cry baby." I said.

"Shut up big head." Ashanti said as she cracked a smile and jumped back into my arms. I passionately kissed her while caressing her body which was turning her on. I slid my hand up under her shirt unstrapping her bra.

"Hold on baby, let me get in the shower." Ashanti said as she backed away from me.

"Come on, we're getting in together." I responded as I grabbed her hand leading her to the shower. I really had to take a moment to get my thoughts together.

I quickly turned around. "Oh shit, I'mma be a daddy!" I said chuckling and I grabbed her again kissing her slowly.

## "Sure to be Watching"

## Aug 31, 2005

I just want to inform y'all that this interview is being recorded. We now have permission of the temporary guardian for Donald Dixon. Mr. Kevin Dixon and his family attorney Richard Dabalowski are also here. Let this interview begin, shall we?" Det. Grove said as he sat beside his partner Det. Banks.

"Mr. Donald Dixon were you the one who initially found your mother Macy Dixon shot to death?" Detective Grove asked.

"Yes, I was." I responded.

"Can you explain to me what you observed before calling 911? Also, where were you coming from that you weren't aware of your mother's death until 9 hours later?" Detective Grove asked.

"The night before I stayed at my uncle's house next to me. Once arriving home, me and my friend found my mother shot to death and we immediately called 911." Don-D responded as the interview went back and forth.

Detective: "Who made the call?"

Don-D: "My friend"

Detective: "And by friend do you mean girlfriend?"

Don-D: "Naw, she's just my friend." Detective: "And you're referring to Miss Ashanti Jackson is that correct?"

Don-D: "Yeah, yup"

Detective: "Do you have any idea who would do this to her or to you by hurting your mother?"

Don-D: "Naw, nope"

Detective: "I know of your cousin Trayvon Dixon aka Trigger Tre.' He's mixed into a lot of different things street wise. Has he mentioned problems he might be tied into?"

Don-D: "Naw"

Detective: "When was the last time you spoke to him?"

Don-D: "Before he went to jail"

Detective: "Did your mother have a male friend or boyfriend?"

Don-D: "Hell naw"

Detective: "We know your dad Sherman Watson is incarcerated in a federal prison. Was anybody looking for him or wanting revenge for anything? Possibly old debts or something?"

Don-D: "Naw" I said. Still not giving any information out.

Detective: "Do you own a Chevrolet Tahoe?"

Don-D: "Yea I do" I answered.

Detective: "Now may I ask what color it is?"

Don-D: "Black"

Detective: "It's black, was it ever any other color?"

Don-D: "Yes, it was white. I got it painted black close to a month ago"

Detective: "You expect me to believe that that wasn't your Tahoe the other day connected with gas station shooting?"

Don-D: "I don't care what you believe there's plenty of Tahoes in this city so you can kiss my ass."

"Okay Detective now if you don't wish to charge my client with anything, I believe it's time we end this interview. Y'all can go protect and serve and start looking for the killer or killers of my client's mother. Other than that, do you two have a development in the case? Because if you want to insinuate anything unrelated you both will do it without my grieving client." Richard Dabalowski said as he interrupted. He didn't even give me a chance to even respond. We stood up heading for the door.

"What's the matter Mr. Dabalowski? We were only asking questions that may be relevant for our ongoing investigation" Det. E. Banks asked.

"No what you're starting to do is harass my client. He told you no once before and you kept it going. If we happen to meet again, I hope the department's questions are more noble than what were just presented. Thank you, detectives. At this point we have to get going. Have a productive day." said my lawyer as he led us to the door and proceeded out.

Once outside my lawyer informed us that he will be in touch within like a week or so. He said to ensure that we could prove that the truck was painted at least days before the shooting. Also, he recommended we get it detailed out. We even got the carpets changed. He told us to stay out of the spotlight because they going to be watching as much as possible.

## "Get to It"

## Aug 31, 2005

I hopped in traffic blasting Jeezy "You ain't perfect" and it was back to the money. I made my way to Auntie's apartment after my lil sex session with my woman.

She was starting to lose her mind. I didn't want that especially while she was carrying my baby. On the other side of things my life and freedom were on the line as Pimp reminded me. Some shit had to be put to a halt soon.

"Hello." I answered the phone.

"What's up Nephew, where you at?" She asked.

"What's up Auntie I was just about to call you I'm pulling in the parking lot right now?" I replied.

"Aight baby I'm unlocking the door right now. Just come on up." Auntie Michelle said.

I pulled out my gun and held it under my shirt. I pressed my duffle bag against it, so it wasn't visible. I always made it a habit to pay attention to detail. I can never move sloppy. Once you start to act loosely or start to smell yourself, the extra attention comes your way. So, it's back to basics day in and day out. You also got to learn the law and statute of limitations. They got five years to the day of your last sell and murders can be tried until your death date.

"Hey baby, how are you doing?" Auntie Michelle said as I walked in the door as I gave her a hug and a kiss on the cheek. I locked the deadbolt on the front door. I placed the Louis Vuitton duffle bag on the couch as I wandered through the house.

"Aye Kevin, where's Keith at?" Auntie asked. She was concerned because during business transactions it was rare to catch him without me or me without him.

"He just had some minor things to take care of that's all." I replied not really wanting to explain the real situation. She didn't deserve an explanation at all. But I stayed cordial. Simply because she could fuck my money up. If she ever tried, I would have to fuck her up. She's a great source of income though so we keep everything wrapped tight with respect around here.

"Oh, okay. I just wanted to make sure he was safe because I'd go to jail about y'all." Auntie Michelle said.

"Oh yeah, he's fine." I replied as I went to the hallway closet to grab my tools.

"Okay so what are we working with today?" Auntie Michelle asked as she grabbed her burnt spoon zippo lighter and some baking soda as she patiently waited for me to get her ready.

"I got 5 zips with me." I replied which is Pittsburgh slang for 5 ounces. I retrieved them from the Louie bag and placed them on the counter.

"Aight let's get my taster ready. Here baby, hold the spoon." Auntie said. She grabbed the cold water, baking soda and lit the lighter. I dropped some cocaine onto the spoon with my free hand. She sprinkled some baking soda on the spoon and started to whip and mix with her pen tip. She kept sprinkling more baking soda to cause it to lock up. She got it in rock form by wetting her fingertips and dripping the cold water onto her spoon. It was a little gummy still so Auntie took it off the spoon and placed it on the countertop to dry.

"Is this from the same batch as the stuff you dropped off last time?" Auntie asked.

"Yeah, yup it is." I replied before Auntie walked out the kitchen and into her bedroom. She came out bringing me the shoe box from under her bed. She struggled to put something in the back pocket of her tight jeans. I turned on my digital scale and started weighing up the different chunks of coke. I needed to know how much soda to add on to each one.

"Iight I'm about to let you know what this shit is hitting for." Auntie said as she grabbed her glass dick. She put her hard in it, put the flame to it so it melted in place and took a blast. The funny smell of crack filled the air as it made the sizzling sound. I watched her take another hit from her pipe before making a popping noise with her lips.

"Kevin sit in the chair." Auntie demanded.

"Huh?" I replied a lil confused because she was not in the position to make commands.

"Kevin sit in the damn chair" Auntie Michelle demanded again as she gave me a lil shove. I did as she said being the fact that she was high. She bent over and started to undo my pants as I looked at her with a funny look.

"What? You are grown right? Just lay back and let me do me. I been wanting to do this for the longest of times." Auntie Michelle said as I lifted up so she could slide my pants down. I sat on my boxers while my pants were at my ankles. The thought of her sucking my dick right after smoking that rock was a turn off so I did what every nigga would do.

"Yo Auntie, you got a condom?" I asked as she immediately pulled it out her back pocket and rolled it down my dick.

"Damn you got a big ass dick." she said before she started to swallow as much as she could. I grabbed the back of her head leading her up and down as she gripped my thighs. She made humming and slurping noises as she continued to handle her business. I came quick and my nut quickly filled up the top part of the condom. Auntie Michelle rolled the condom off as she caught my nut and proceeded to keep going on. She sent my eyes rolling as she played with my balls with her hand. She had me aroused all over again. She kept going until I nutted again. At this point it wasn't too much coming out, but she swallowed that too.

"Damn girl. You made my shoes come off." I said as I had realized that my right shoe came off while she was doing her thing. We laughed because I didn't even remember kicking it off.

"Some good head will do that. Well look I'm about to go wash my mouth out." Auntie Michelle said as she left the kitchen.

"Aight well I'm about to get my Chef Boyardee on." I responded as I stood up fixing my clothes then headed over to the sink. I got myself together, washed my dick off then washed my hands. I went back in the kitchen and started cooking up the coke.

My total was solid. It was six ounces straight up and down as I cut back on the soda a lil. Trying not to stretch it so much also knowing the profit lies in the extras. But if you lose da quality, you'll eventually lose the customer because a fiend trying to get high will never owe you no loyalty especially when their spending the money with you.

I put the money from the shoe box inside my Louie duffle bag and figured I'd go back home. I needed to count the money up so I could split up me and Don-D's bread. I planned to go link with Trigga Tre' and Bad News once I finished. We about to make something happen to get rid of these niggas. When I made it back to the crib, I could see the stress still on Ashanti's face. I immediately went over and gave her a long hug and a kiss.

"What's up babe, you good?" I asked.

"Yes, I'm okay. I was about to make something to eat. What do you want to eat Boo?" Ashanti asked me.

"Oh naw, I just want you to sit down and count this money for me while I make you something to eat. I don't want you to be on your feet all day. We going to do this pregnancy right." I said. I made Ashanti light up because I was showing sensitivity to her and the pregnancy. While I was in the kitchen making Ashanti's food, I got a call on my cell phone from Trigga Tre'.

"Yo, what's smacking' cuz?" I asked.

"Shit I just got word from one of my youngins that the niggas been looking for your whereabouts. Whenever you get a chance make your way to my baby mom's spot and I'll meet you there." Trigga Tre' instructed me.

"Bet I'll pull up in about two hours. I'm in the middle of some shit with Ashanti." I responded.

"Iight nigga handle your B.I. just let me know when you on your way so I can be on my way you dig?" Trigga Tre' said. We locked in the plans and hung up the phone.

I was just about finished cooking the meal I had started. "Iight here you go babe. It's shrimp alfredo over fresh cut fries." I informed her as I placed the food on the table. This was one of the six meals I could put together that was actually good.

"Oh, thank you baby!" she responded. Me and Ashanti ate and just relaxed for a moment. We loved all on each other and catered to one another's needs. After a couple hours she was sleep with her head on my lap. I decided to leave a note on the table and take off.

I knew that tonight was the last night I'd be able to drive the rental. The police will have a description of the vehicle by tomorrow morning. I figured I would take it to Don-D and Uncle Kev. I hit Trigga Tre' telling him I was on my way. Don-D hit me telling me about his interview with the detectives. His family lawyer suggested to him that he kept a low profile. He warned him that the jakes was about to be on his ass and I agreed. I had to think of a way to keep him out of the spotlight and out of harm's way all in the same breath.

"Yo, I been waiting on you, come on let's head up." Tre' said as he and Bad News was hopping out of his '94 Caprice Classic. We went up to Jamaya's spot.

"I got a chance to talk to Don-D a lil ago. They were asking a lot of questions like they were onto something. I'm going to send him, Lexi, and Ashanti on a little vacation just until everything finished. Ashanti just told me she pregnant so I ain't trying to stress her out with all the shit here." I said.

"I can dig it. Congratulations too bro." Gutta-Gutta said as they both shook my hand.

"Good looking. Iight so let's get down to business. What's goodie?" I asked.

"This bitch I be fucking named Toni from the Hill District overheard the nigga Biggie asking one of her girlfriends about what you do. She was trying to figure out who you be with too. She called to tell me about where the nigga's crib is. So, what you want to do?" Trigga Tre' asked me.

"Bet, we going in there tonight. Aye Gutta-Gutta I need you to you to go to McKeesport or Clairton and get a hottie. We gone use that because I'm putting some diabolical shit together. I don't want these bodies to show up in the city or forever for that matter. We gone ride out tonight" I informed.

"Aight bet, well we about to slide out to get that joint now. You gone post here until we get back or you got some other shit to do?" Trigga Tre' asked.

"I'm posted for like a half until I get in touch with my connect" I responded.

"Say less, Jamaya should be here soon to keep you company. We out." Trigga Tre' said before they walked out the front door. I immediately squawked Pimp so I could holla at him.

"What's up Neph?" Pimp said.

"Ay Unc I need to holla at you." I responded.

"Squawk me back in 15 minutes." Pimp said as I sat there in the crib for a couple minutes. Jamaya came walking in the door with lil Tre' sleep in her arms. She waved at us and put him in his bed came back into the living room to chill with me.

"I seen your fake baby mama today." Jamaya said sarcastically before continuing as I just shook my head.

"She wants me to call her. She asked about you and she told me that you and ya woman cursed her out on the phone." Jamaya informed.

"Yeah, that bitch is straight loco. I don't know what the fuck is wrong with her." I replied.

"I'm about to call her. You got a couple minutes to spare or you about to leave?" She asked me as she pulled out her phone.

"Naw not yet, go head and call her." I responded as she dialed Kayla's number with her picking up on the third ring.

"Hello" Kayla said answering the phone all bothered.

"Kayla, what's up girl?" Jamaya responded engaging into conversation.

"Jamaya, hey girl what's up with you?" Kayla replied.

"Shit just getting to the crib with lil Tre' what you up to?" Jamaya asked.

"I'm just getting off the damn bus. I'm on my way to my momma's house." Kayla told her.

"Damn that's crazy. I can't believe that shit you told me about Shawn! Like he really acted like that." Jamaya said acting shocked.

"Yeah, it's cool though. I got his black ass when I see him" Kayla responded as she kept rambling on about the baby being mines. She kept talking about how she wants our family together. It just gave me confirmation on how delusional she really is. She was believing all the lies she put in her own head.

Shortly after they hung up the phone Pimp squawked me back. He told me to stop past Spot A, Spot X and then Spot B. This meant I had to stop at his sister's house, then to Wal-Mart parking lot before ending up at Pimp's mother's house.

Pimp had two of his bitches come outside and meet me. They escorted me in the house and to where he was.

"What's up Unc?" I greeted him.

"Hold up Neph. Have a seat." He said while he walked over to ol' girl.

"Bitch what the fuck did I just say? Don't make me repeat myself. Bitch you're running on ocean water. That means you about to drown with me. If I turn green somebody going to turn purple." Pimp said as he stood up talking through his teeth at one of his females as she took off running. She went on to do what she was told screaming yes daddy!

Everybody left the room besides Barbie which was Pimp's main bitch. She was kind of like the dog that hurdles the sheep. She sat at the table with us.

"What's up Neph?" Pimp asked.

"I want to get rid of some problems the best way possible. The water just ain't making sense for me this go around. You know eventually the closet opens and skeletons pop out." I said.

"I understand. Barbie get Justin on the phone and tell him to schedule a couple of funerals. Shawn, I'm giving you 48 hours (about 2 days) to handle your business because this is my genie in the bottle. When I have a problem, he covers it up. He *also* makes sure it never comes back to haunt me. You tuned in Neph?" Pimp asked.

"Yeah yup, I'm following you Unc." I responded.

# NAME OF DA GAME

"Justin works at a cemetery and gives infamous funerals for me. After he heats up the lye, it dissolves a body at 350 degrees within 3 hours. You got literally 48 hours max, go handle your business." Pimp said as Barbie just walked back into the room.

"It's done daddy." Barbie said.

"Okay I need you to stop past spot A, then past F spot and get you something to eat. When you leave, meet Barbie at spot M. You still remember how to get there right?" Pimp asked me referring to his weapons castle.

"Yeah, I remember Unc." I responded after jogging my memory for a few seconds. It had honestly been a few months since Pimp showed me that spot.

"Iight, well get to it" Pimp said as he left the room. I left the crib and went about my day.

## "He Gone, Fuck!"

## Aug 31, 2005

I met Barbie and loaded the fuck up. I grabbed a blacked-out AB-10 with the fifty-round clip, an army fatigue Carbon-15 that holds .223's, and a chrome AK-47 fully automatic. I pulled three bulletproof vests with the bulletproof head gear. The same gear that SWAT has. After situating everything, I made my way back to Jamaya's house.

Bad News told me that they had got a Dodge Plymouth Van and took the liberty of taking the middle row out for us. They tucked the van in a garage around the corner. It was in an alley not too far from here. I was comfortable with the plan at hand. I got on the internet and scheduled a flight to Las Vegas for Ashanti, Lexi, and Don-D. I booked two rooms at the Palms Casino Resort. Their flight was scheduled to leave in 3 hours. Once everything was situated, I linked all three of them and told them about their flight. They was cool but sick I wasn't coming along.

I reassured them I was going to be okay. They understood that business needed to be taken care of here. Once everything calms down I'll bring them back home. I feel this was a rainy day so I sent Ashanti to round up $24,000 of my money. I slid them 8 grand each and if more was needed I would Western Union. Don-D was too young for the casinos, and they didn't play that fake age shit at all. Money wasn't nothing so I would of gave them as much as they wanted. Ashanti and Lexi stopped past Jamaya's crib once their bags were packed. I gave Ashanti a quickie in Jamaya's bathroom. We washed up and got it together, but I knew she'd be leaking an hour later.

They headed to the airport around 8pm to get ready to board their flight. It was starting to get dark which was perfect for us. Me, Trigga Tre, and Bad News booted up and followed the directions to Biggie's house. We parked a little further down the street to scope. We wanted to check out the place and to watch for any traffic going in and out cribs. We also needed to scope out the Dope Boys.

We sat outside watching the house drinking Gatorades, eating Cheetos, and smoking Newport 100's. Niggas even had Gatorade bottles to piss in as we staked out until 4:30 a.m. We figured the traffic would be wrapped up around then. We threw on our head gear, Isotoner gloves, long sleeved Under Armour and all grabbed our guns of choice. Trigga Tre' took the AB-10 and Gutta-Gutta was a tweak for the choppa. I found a certain rush going through my body with the Carbon-15 in my hands.

Gutta-Gutta started the van and we drove down the back alley. It gave us easier access to the back of the house. We all left our cell phones in the van just in case we dropped one. If so, it could be traced back to us or someone close to us. To avoid any fuck ups, we left everything in the ride. The only way we wouldn't make it back is if we died first.

Once in the alley Trigga Tre' got out and approached the back door. He squatted down as we spun back around to the front of the house. We parked a bit closer to the crib and approached the front door. We all had on digital watches set to the same time. We were all set to kick the door in exactly at 4:40a.m sharp. It also gave the illusion that we're the cops because this is how they hit spots.

It was a solid plan. The crib is between two abandoned houses. We shut the door behind us to defuse the chances of someone calling the cops. We slimmed the chances down to like 50%. Mainly because this is the hood and gun shots rang out all the time. They rarely ever called the cops around this way if it didn't directly involve them. Nine times out of 10, they were going to turn the other cheek.

Gutta-Gutta kicked the door in and I followed him in. Once inside I could see Trigga directly across from me standing in the kitchen. We all got low as we could hear someone's footsteps coming down from upstairs. B-Nasty appeared from around the corner shirtless. Trigga Tre hit him three times as soon as he came in the kitchen. I hit him once dropping him. His body twisted on his way to the ground and his Uzi started to spray for a couple seconds. It ended up putting like 30 bullet holes in the wall. We searched every inch of every room. I wasn't leaving unless everybody was DOA. With the basement being empty we made our way up the steps and we stepped over B-Nasty's body. He was leaking blood all over trying to gasp for air. We proceeded to the second floor where it was only two bedrooms and a bathroom.

Nasty obviously came from the room on the left being the door was left open. There was another Uzi clip on the dresser. I searched this room high and low from under the bed to all the bullshit in the closet. I made sure there wasn't anyone hiding behind the clothes.

We went across the hall to the other bedroom Trigga Tre kicked it open but wasn't quick enough because Biggie busted two shots hitting him in his head gear making him fall. Bad News started chopping him down as he let off about 20 shots. It was close I couldn't hear out my right ear for a minute. I mean that shit was loud as fuck.

"You bitch ass nigga that's my fuckin Baby Da..." started to yell DaVita before I popped her four times. I let off six shots and four of them hit her right in the head. Her neck flew back in a jerking motion before her body dropped to the floor. She was missing half of her face. Both of their pools of blood began to run together.

I walked to the closet as everybody continued search the room. I kicked back the closet door and seen a little ass boy who couldn't be no older than two years old scared to death. He was crying and shaking when Trigga Tre' raised his pistol ad smacked the shit out of the little boy. He hit him so hard I thought he killed him.

"Naw I'm going to kill this lil fucker." Trigga Tre' said as we both held him back before Bad News intervened.

"Naw, chill let the lil nigga ride. His life already gone be fucked up. Come on let's get these bodies out of here." he said before grabbing my arms. We started to slide bodies toward the steps as I looked down and noticed B-Nasty was gone.

"Yo, he's gone!" I yelled to them as I ran down the steps looking for B-Nasty. The front door was wide open and the Impala that had been parked directly in front of the door was gone.

"He's gone. Fuck man." Bad News yelled as he could see the trail of blood leaving out of the front door. I walked over and shut the front door and went back upstairs to quickly move the bodies downstairs to the van.

## "What's Death Like?"

## Sept. 1, 2005

I heard a choppa going off. Those were the sounds that brought me back from out of it. My body was so weak as I can feel myself bleeding out. I think I'm still breathing because of all the liquor in my system. I immediately heard DaVita yelling followed by a few loud booms and the screaming stopped at that point. I knew it was over for them as it took everything in me to get up. I could not feel or move my left side. I checked to make sure it was still intact with my body. Shit felt like it had been blown completely off.

I wanted to go upstairs and war it out. But I knew if I did not get out this house before they came back downstairs, I would die. I feel the only reason I'm not dead (them coming to finish me off) is because they already think I'm dead. I began to pull myself together slowly so that I could reach for my brother's keys to the whip. I crawled over to the car door and used it as leverage to stand myself up.

## NAME OF DA GAME

I started stumbling and falling into the car barely making it there. It took everything in me. By the time I sped two blocks away, I realized my whole driver's seat was drenched in my own blood. I pulled over and tried not to panic as I was going in and out of it. I was able to grab a shirt that was in the back seat as I wrapped my dead arm in it to keep pressure on it. I reached out to the only person whose number I knew by heart.

"Hey Bro." Shariece said as she picked up the phone sounding like she was still grieving about my brother. I took a gulp from the Hennessy bottle that I had from earlier.

"Reese I just got shot. I think I'm about to die hurry please I'm on Jackson." I was able to force it out before I went out of it. Shariece was still talking through the phone as she tried to communicate. My silence made her start screaming.

"Oh my God, B hold on! Here I come, please don't die on me." Shariece voice started to fade completely away. I suddenly couldn't hear her anymore. I couldn't see the streetlight in front of me. I thought to myself this is what death must feel like.

## "Getting Rid of Problems"

## Sept. 1, 2005

D amn I can't believe that nigga wasn't dead." I said angrily as we drove over to the Lawrenceville entrance to the Allegheny Cemetery. Pimp told us Justin would be awaiting our arrival. His only purpose for being there is to let us in to dump the bodies. You know to get rid of these problems for life.

"From this moment forward, we over kill everything. Nothing gets less than 15 slugs! All these niggas taking these bullets like 'Pac or Fif'." Gutta-Gutta said as we drove into the cemetery. Justin stood there next to three open graves.

"Aye, bring the bodies over here. Dump one in this one and the other in that one" Justin said. He was an unshaved pot belly white man who had to be in his late 40's or early 50's.

We did as he said and then drove over to the Hill District where we changed our clothes and dumped the soiled ones into the can. We poured gasoline all over the inside of the van. We doused a tee shirt in it too. We set it on fire in a dead-end alley way before we drove off. Now all that was left to do was find our missing man.

# NAME OF DA GAME

I needed to go get some sleep right now though. I was so tired my eyes were killing me. I took the weapons and bulletproof gear back to Pimp's weapon castle. I followed his route to spot A, spot D, and spot M.

## "I Ain't Going Alone"

## Sept. 1, 2005

O h my God, he's alive." Shariece said as she stood over me smiling through the tears that fell down her eyes.

"What happened?" was all I could ask as my body was in so much pain and I noticed all the machines around me. Dr. Doc stood over top of me with a chart in his hand. He continued to check my vitals making sure I was okay before finally telling me about myself.

"B, I don't know how to tell you all this. I'll start with the good news and then bad. First off, you're alive and I'm quite certain you're going to live through this and see a full recovery. By the time she got you here you had only 2 quarts of blood in your body. I had to figure out your blood type and call in a favor to a close friend from the Red Cross. A recovery of this magnitude is going to take you three to six months depending on how your body heals.

# NAME OF DA GAME

The only things I am concerned about is your left arm and your whole right side is paralyzed. I estimate a year or two of physical therapy should have it back functioning. Even though your mobility isn't fully restored, most of it will be. I'll add that if it weren't for Shariece finding you when she did you would have bled to death. The alcohol you had consumed prolonged it and kept your blood flowing. She wrapped up your wounds and kept you from going into shock until I got here.

"Thanks girl." I said to Shariece as everything just sounded so unreal to my ears. I just felt a sense of love from a higher power to be alive.

"No problem ugly. I'm glad you ain't die on me" Shariece said.

"I'm cool. You don't have to worry about me. I'm a G." I responded.

"Is that right?" Shariece replied before cracking a little smile at me as I gave one back.

"So how you get me in here?" B-Nasty asked.

"My girl Kayla helped me. She had to leave earlier because she was going to Ohio for a fashion show. You'll meet her one day when she comes down South Carolina to visit us." Shariece informed.

"To visit who? I am not going down no mothafuckin South Carolina!" B snapped back.

"Well why the fuck not, huh? You just want to keep your ass up here fighting and shooting? These niggas obviously know more about y'all than y'all do them. Y'all just plan to keep going back and forth until you're all dead? It makes no sense! You sound really dumb right now. Like real fuckin dumb!" Shariece snapped on me.

"B she's right, it's not safe to be here right now. You're in no health to do anything, especially to retaliate. I think you should go down there with her." Dr. Doc jumped in.

"But why South Carolina?" I asked.

"Because I got a bomb ass job offer down there. My Nana died two years ago and left her house to me. So that's where we are going." Shariece responded.

"South Carolina it is then." I obliged.

"Okay so I cleaned out the car because we can't take it with us. The police will be looking for you now since your blood and fingerprints were all over that house. They will come for you first since they have no answers and no bodies.

"No bodies?" I repeated back as it didn't register the first time it was said to me.

"No, they took the bodies too." Shariece responded. I knew in this instant that the game had no rules and they meant business.

"When are we leaving?" I asked.

"Doc said to give him a week or two for monitoring to make sure you're cool. I already had your mom pack some of your things. I got the U-Haul coming tomorrow. They contracted a company to help us move for an extra fee. Are you ready?" I asked.

"What about my mom and all my money? I got a whole key of dope out in my hide out spot." I informed.

"We going to get all your money and I don't know what you plan to do with the dope. I mean if you want I can try to get it off wholesale for you because its going to be a while not unless you want to take it with us and you sit on it but with you trynna recover and trusting new people that's really a lot" Reese informed.

"Naw I'd rather sale it now, I can always get back with my plug another day" I uttered out.

Well going to try to sell it today or tomorrow to some Detroit niggas. I know they have the dough and don't always wanna go all the way back, so what do you want for it?" Reese asked.

# NAME OF DA GAME

"Tell them to just give me 60k and it's taking a three too." But take somebody with you because people will kill you for all of that. I answered.

"Okay I got you just rest up and I'll be back as soon as I can." Reese replied.

"Say less, here go the key to the apartment. The address is 6 Columbo Street. Go up on the second floor and go into the bedroom to the left. In the closet is a gun safe with duffle bag. The combination is 8-35-14. The dope is the same bedroom in the refrigerator." I said as I laid there putting all of my trust, I had in her. Any other time I wouldn't have done it. But I owe her trust to some extent. She earned that in my books.

"Okay I'm about to leave. The police got little Chris because he was in the house. I heard they got him down at CYS. Biggie and DaVita had money at both of their mama's houses so whoever gets him will be set. DaVita's mom said they got 80 grand there. Biggie's mom is too hurt she ain't even start to count it. She said it's two duffle bags though. She just wants her son's body." Shariece informed me. I was hurt for all the losses I had to take in the last couple of days. I know once I'm well they will see me again. I put that on my brother because I ain't dead yet. And I ain't going alone when I do. □

## "The World is Yours"

## March 13, 2006

I'm gone tear that pussy up." played the Young Jeezy song as we sat in the V.I.P. section of a Dallas Strip Club. Texas was always a vibe.

"Ay Neph come over here, let me holla at you for a second." Pimp said.

"What's up Unc?" I responded.

"Look I don't know how to say this other than I'm proud of you Sales. I'm turning 38 in eight days and the games been good to me. I got eight kids and I feel you're ready to be the man in our city. You never really know how somebody is cut and what they'll do. You don't how they'll handle situations until it comes their way. From what you've shown me I feel it's time to pass over the crown of king of the city. I'm going to introduce you to my connect when we get home. I've already told him about you. I dumped those keys on you to see if you rise to the pressure that I put on you. You showed me and proved to me that you have what it takes. You stayed so low. You really about this life Neph."

"Good look Unc. I won't let you down, I got you."

"I know Neph, the world is truly yours now." Pimp said as we continued to party the night away Texas was always a vibe.

"How you feeling Neph?" Pimp asked me.

"I'm good Unc" I replied as took a sip of my bottle of grey goose.

"You sure Neph?" Pimp asked again making me double back on my thoughts.

"Yea it's been a long ride though" I replied.

"You right Neph, shit not all fun and games but you know the name of the game, and what it takes to get it done, plan to the end, and crush your enemies at all cost. Never let that bullshit to happen like that ever again be strong and secure in all your actions and movements. It's always chess not checkers and never forget it" Pimp said preaching to me in the middle of the club.

"I can't and I won't" I said as I tapped the tattoo my left forearm of Momma Mace and tribute me and Don-D had got together in her memory.

"I hear you Neph, and I hope so, we'll talk some more soon but enjoy your night and have some fun" Pimp instructed me before shaking my hand and propping down in his seat as he basically was just over seeing us as he had 4 of his hoes all around him.

I needed a good unwind with all that had been going on, and really pressing the area, had to knock off two of their youngins who were trynna ride and a couple more got hit up severely, in which I think they got the message. There are like 5 major figures that are locked up across the country that might give static but won't be able to check their temperatures until they are home. The money we've been making through them phones and area been a goldmine. And like nothing we used to for sure. Putting way more people in position to get some money.

Shifting focus back to these females down D-town. Alot of these females was thick as hell and looked and shined like they had their own money. They had bottles, sections, and was throwing money on the strippers too. The night it was winding down and it was time to key in on something.

Ashanti was with Lexi down D.C. enjoying some National Cherry Blossom festival that was about to take place. The food and scenery would be enough to keep things relaxed on her end for a little while and bonding with her sister as they got closer over the pregnancy. She was staying there for the last couple days before she moves to South Carolina with D-Weez and her son Malik.

"Ya'll cool?" I asked as I approached a circle with my boys as they all were smiling, drinking, smoking, and tossing money on the strippers.

"Yea niggaz is livin" Trigga Tre responded as we fist bumped and continued to engage with the females.

We partied until it closed and which by that time, we had all picked who we were fucking with for the night and was off to get something to eat before getting the hotel suites.

"Come on let me holla at ya'll right quick before we all disappear and play holy matrimony for the night." Pimp hollered out as he did his diddy bop to the middle of the hallway like he was Tom Brady getting ready for the game winning drive.

"What's up Unc?" I responded as we all gathered around Pimp.

"So let me tell ya'll this story real quick, because I ain't have a chance to say it earlier" Pimp stated as he made sure he had all our eyes and ears before proceeding on.

"So I got on the phone and called Star the other day she picked up the phone like yes daddy, I said hoe go and get a pencil and paper and come back to the phone, she was like yes daddy and disappeared away from the phone and came back like 15 seconds later and was like Daddy I got a pen and paper and then I looked at the phone and said hoe I said a pencil, she replied yes Daddy and disappeared again, once she came back to the phone again she was like ok Daddy I got a pencil, I was like good, now is it sharpened she replied yes Daddy, now break the pencil in half, she gone repeat like break the pencil in half and I snapped like Bitch did I studder, she was like yes Daddy I did it, so I say now throw the part with the eraser in the trash, I did Daddy, good, now do you know what that means, no Daddy I don't, That means no more mistakes hoe, now let's get it together every day is game 7" Pimp said to us with a straight face before just turning and walking off.

Halfway making it to where his hoes was Pimp turned around doing a 360 in one swift motion pointing and looking at us "The world is yours" and kept it moving again with his George Jefferson walk.

"I know I had different plans when I first jumped in the game. Shit changed up and I was sucked in. I'm almost 18 and I'm expecting my first seed next week. I got all I need and more around me. I can't complain, I'm truly up. As of now my problems are solved. My teams right and we all 100." I said.

I'll tell you the rest of the story in sequel titled 'Da Game Don't Change". Until then be true to who you are and what you stand for. Keep your priorities in line and keep your mind focused. The rest will come. You can have power, bitches, and money.... But loyalty, a great name and family are everything and that's irreplaceable. Always remember that.

Blacc

www.ingramcontent.com/pod-product-compliance
Lightning Source LLC
Chambersburg PA
CBHW050348030726
47503CB00008B/2666